NOT AS A COWARD

Adele Price, after a sheltered Victorian upbringing with her kindly aunt and uncle in Wiltshire, longs for a challenge in life. Then she meets Philip Belvedere, and after a whirlwind courtship, they marry. Philip takes her back to Sadura, his home town in south-west India, and Adele is indeed challenged. The house is dominated by Philip's old ayah, and Philip's behaviour seems strange and deceitful. Meanwhile, it's David Baxter, the local doctor, who helps Adele to face her troubles . . .

Books by Lillie Holland
in the Linford Romance Library:

LOVE'S ALIEN SHORE
THE ECHOING BELLS
AFTER THE HARVEST

LILLIE HOLLAND

◆

NOT AS A COWARD

Complete and Unabridged

LINFORD
Leicester

First published in Great Britain in 1976

First Linford Edition
published 2012

British Library CIP Data

Holland, Lillie.
   Not as a coward.- -(Linford romance library)
   1. Love stories.
   2. Large type books.
   I. Title II. Series
   823.9'2–dc23

   ISBN 978–1–4448–1323–4

Published by
F. A. Thorpe (Publishing)
Anstey, Leicestershire

Set by Words & Graphics Ltd.
Anstey, Leicestershire
Printed and bound in Great Britain by
T. J. International Ltd., Padstow, Cornwall

This book is printed on acid-free paper

1

With a mixture of love and exasperation I watched Uncle Henry's plump, pink forefinger go carefully over the map of India. It came to rest on the south-west tip.

'The climate there must be very bad, Mr — er — Belvedere.' His eyes met Philip's dark ones.

'Not always, sir. It's quite cool, pleasant, in fact, from December to February. There are times, of course, when it becomes very hot. But when it does, some of the wives go up to the Hills.'

'H'm.'

Uncle Henry did not sound convinced. He exchanged a worried glance with Aunt Margaret.

I loved them, of course; I didn't want to leave them, but I had to marry Philip Belvedere — I simply had to! Why couldn't they understand; why couldn't they see? For a few moments we all sat silent in the drawing room of Onger House, our charming home in Wiltshire. Aunt Margaret had always given me to understand that they hoped I would marry one day. 'Make a suitable match', was the way she put it. Well, what was a suitable match? Philip Belvedere was young, handsome, and a gentleman, even though he had been educated in India. He had a nice house there, and a flourishing tile factory. But the factory seemed to be a stumbling block, too.

'He's in trade, Adele,' my aunt had said, after his means of livelihood had been disclosed.

'Aunt Margaret, is that a crime? Don't you see, things are changing? A great many people from very good backgrounds are in trade these days — '

'Things are different in India, I suppose,' broke in Uncle Henry. 'As Adele says, it is possible these days to be in trade, and yet still be a gentleman.

After all, it is right and proper that we should develop our Empire. It isn't that point I'm worried about.'

'What is then, Uncle?' I asked.

'Well, my dear, you've led a very sheltered life. How long have you known this young man? Barely three months. He's been spending a few months here on holiday, and you want to marry him and go back to India. A young girl, alone in a foreign country — where would you turn for help, should the need arise?'

'Uncle!' I cried in exasperation. 'I would have my husband! How would I be alone?'

'But you are not mature enough to judge character, Adele. It is so easy for any young man to be gay and charming while he is on holiday. You don't know — you can't possibly know what living in India is like . . . '

These were the arguments which went on almost daily in our house, ever since I had said that Philip would be speaking to Uncle Henry. And now he had spoken to Uncle Henry, and formally asked his permission to marry me.

After dinner, Aunt Margaret and I had withdrawn, and left the two men alone together.

I sat down in the drawing room and picked up some embroidery. Aunt Margaret sat facing me in her wing chair. After a few minutes I put down the embroidery and walked over to the piano. I ran my fingers across the keys.

'Don't fidget so, Adele,' said my aunt, peevishly. 'If you want to play, play.'

She was not irritable as a rule, but I knew that she was as tensed up as I was. Suppose there was an argument — suppose Uncle Henry got into a 'state', as she called it? When he was upset he would go alarmingly red in the face. I couldn't bear to see my uncle upset, but I loved Philip — I loved him.

I sat down and played *Oh For The Wings Of A Dove*. Perhaps it was not the happiest of choices, but it happened to be the piece of music up on the piano.

'Yes, you may play that now,' said my aunt. 'But you might be wishing for the wings of a dove to fly back to us. Oh, I know you don't care about us now — '

I jumped off the piano stool, and put my arm round Aunt Margaret's shoulders. 'Don't talk like that — please,' I whispered, fighting back the tears. 'I don't want to go away and leave you and Uncle Henry. But I love Philip — I'd go anywhere in the world with him. Can't you understand, Aunt?'

'Yes, Adele,' she said sadly. 'I understand. But you don't understand the way of the world, nor how precious you are to us.'

I had lost both my parents when very young, and my childless aunt and uncle had brought me up. They were not wealthy, but they were not poor, either, and I had not lacked for anything throughout my childhood and girlhood.

I was torn between my love for them, and this passion which had swept into my life so quickly. I had been staying with my other aunt, Mary, in London, and while I was there, I had attended several balls and functions with my twenty-year-old cousin, Sophie.

It was at one of these that I had been introduced to Philip Belvedere. I thought he was the most handsome and charming young man I had ever met.

When we first waltzed together I felt quite tongue-tied. He smiled at me all the time.

'Does it hurt?' he asked anxiously.

'Does what hurt?'

'Your eyes. They tip up a bit at the corners.'

It was an absurd remark, but somehow it put me at my ease. With his arm around me, I felt as if I were dancing on a cloud. I wanted the music to go on and on. I had always believed in love at first sight, and now I knew it was true.

The trouble was, Aunt Margaret had discouraged too much vanity at home, as she thought it was slightly sinful.

'Beauty is only skin-deep,' she used to say. 'A nice disposition is far more important.' Somehow it sounded rather dull though. And how could people fall in love at first sight with someone who only had a nice disposition?

As a child I had been a plain, rather mousy looking little girl, but over the past two years or so, I had blossomed out surprisingly. Several people had remarked on it, which had worried my aunt, for fear my head would be turned.

And now, here was this young man with beautiful, black, wavy hair, and long-lashed dark eyes, whispering compliments and charming remarks right at the beginning of our acquaintanceship.

I hardly slept at all after that first ball. Sophie and I drank hot chocolate in bed, and talked together. But eventually she fell asleep, while I lay wakeful until the dawn.

'You won't see him again,' Sophie had remarked, with a yawn. 'Oh, he's handsome and agreeable and charming, and all the girls are agog if he so much as looks at them. But he is only in England on holiday from India, and merely wants to have a good time by all accounts. Your head is quite turned because he danced with you, Adele. And told you a lot of nonsense, no doubt.'

Perhaps. But he hadn't danced at all with Sophie, and I knew that underneath, she was nettled.

The following day he called and asked Aunt Mary if he could take Sophie and me out driving. Flustered, my aunt didn't know what to do. Finally she consented, but wrote an anxious letter to her sister in Wiltshire. Because straight away, by some mysterious instinct, Aunt Mary knew that I was the one Philip Belvedere was interested in, not her daughter.

Sophie was very pretty, with glossy brown ringlets, and round, pink cheeks, but I was the one he wanted, there was no doubt about that. He was respectful and charming, but he was persistent. Uncle Henry and Aunt Margaret soon found themselves entertaining him.

And now, after a whirlwind courtship, he was trying to get Uncle Henry

not merely to consent to an engagement, but to allow us to marry before
he sailed back to India in July . . .

Uncle Henry's forefinger was still
resting on the southwest tip of India.

'I could come back for long holidays,'
I said, a catch in my throat. I had a
horrible fear that my aunt and uncle
and I would all dissolve into tears any
moment. If Uncle would only say one
way or the other . . . He looked at me,
and I knew in that moment that I had
won. But how sad his blue eyes were.

'Very well.' He sighed deeply. 'Someone must take care of you, Adele. I
knew this would happen one day. But I
didn't think it would be happening so
soon — or that you would be going
abroad — ' He broke off.

Aunt Margaret and I both began to
cry, and Philip looked very embarrassed. So although I was madly happy
at having my uncle's consent to our
marriage, I had some very mixed-up
emotions at leaving home. After we had
dried our tears, my uncle sent for a

bottle of champagne, and, rather solemnly, we all drank to our future happiness.

Plans went forward for the wedding. Philip had produced a rather faded photograph of the house 'Lebanon' where he would be taking me as his bride. It looked charming, standing high on a stepped plinth, with a wide verandah running round it. Lebanon — my future home!

'Well, it looks very nice, I'm sure,' said Aunt Margaret. For some time she peered at it through a magnifying glass. Then she passed it to Uncle Henry.

'Where is the — er — tile factory?' enquired my uncle.

'You can't see it on that photograph. The factory is down the creek and round the corner,' said Philip.

'It is — I suppose — flourishing?'

'There is always a demand for tiles,' was the bland reply. I knew that Philip did not care for Uncle Henry to ask him questions like that. Nor did I, for that matter. I knew that for my sake he would not be rude to my aunt and uncle, but there were times when their endless questions and comments embarrassed me and annoyed him. I met his eyes, and smiled encouragingly.

After all, they had given their consent to our marriage, and we could afford to be magnanimous. Aunt Margaret talked a great deal about how little I knew of life, and how harsh it could be. What my aunt didn't know — what nobody really understood — was that I didn't want just an ordinary, everyday sort of life such as she envisaged for me. I wanted something more, something different. Exciting things were happening in the world, and I wanted to be part of them. I knew Aunt Margaret would have looked askance at me if I had said that I wanted adventure.

She would have thought it a most unseemly idea. What were things coming to, when a girl wanted adventure? She would never believe that times were changing, and that my generation of girls had different ideas.

Life at Onger House was very tranquil; my aunt and I tatted and embroidered, and did charitable work. We also had At Homes, and exchanged visits with our neighbours. There were pleasant house parties, balls, and exciting stays at Cousin Sophie's in London.

Philip had been staying with a family who had apparently been friendly with his father years before, the Pritchards.

My aunt and uncle knew them slightly.

'Mrs Pritchard is the biggest gossip I know,' Aunt Margaret remarked, during one of our long drawn out discussions concerning my future with Philip. 'She makes it her business to find out other people's, and then she passes on the information. Your Aunt Mary doesn't care for her, either. No doubt Philip would enjoy himself at their house; the two Pritchard sons lead quite a gay life, and there would be many invitations forthcoming.'

'Yes, he was with both the young men

at the function where we met,' I explained. 'Mrs Pritchard was there, chaperoning the eldest daughter. Sophie and I were together — '

'But surely your Aunt Mary was there too?' A look of disbelief sprang into my aunt's eyes.

'Er — well, she would have been, but she was not feeling very well, and Sophie and I begged to go — '

'You mean Mr Belvedere — er — Philip actually met you unchaperoned at a ball? Small wonder that he called at the house the following day! Did you hear that?' Aunt Margaret turned to her husband.

'Oh, well,' muttered Uncle Henry, 'doubtless Mary didn't want to disappoint the girls.'

'We came to no harm,' I put in.

My aunt still looked disapproving. 'Your father knew the Pritchards years ago,' she went on. 'Mrs Pritchard would certainly prick up her ears when she knew that her young guest had met Miss Adele Price.'

'I don't see how her tongue could wag about me,' I said with a trace of impatience.

Aunt Margaret compressed her lips still further. But I was thinking that marrying Philip was going to give me the chance of adventure, and the freedom I had secretly longed for. And because I knew that I was going to get my own way, I listened patiently to the advice my aunt bestowed on me. For years we had shared the same lady's maid, Eunice.

'Naturally, it is out of the question for Eunice to accompany you to India, Adele. But you must have a maid, and a good one. We must advertise.'

I mentioned this to Philip as we strolled through the gardens at Onger House. It was spring, but hot enough for any summer day. I was wearing a gown of white muslin, and carrying a tiny, be-frilled parasol.

'It's so hot,' I remarked, as we sat down on a rustic garden seat.

Philip laughed. 'If you call this hot,

what will you think it is at Sadura?'

'Hotter, I suppose. Can you hear the cuckoo in the woods over there? What will it be like now, in Sadura?'

'Terrible,' said Philip. 'It's the hot season, before the rains come.'

'I've been thinking,' I said. 'I had better advertise for a maid, Philip. I can't take Eunice away from Aunt Margaret, even if she would be willing to come — '

'You don't need a maid,' he cut in quite sharply. 'The ayah will look after you.'

'The ayah?' I repeated.

'Yes. She cared for me from being quite young. After my mother died, she brought me up. As you know, my father never married again.'

'But . . . surely an ayah's a nurse-maid,' I said slowly. 'What would you and your father want with an ayah in the house after you were grown up?'

'She's always been there — she's done everything. I suppose you would call her a housekeeper in England. It

15

simply isn't necessary to take an English maid out with us.'

For a moment I sat without speaking. It was unthinkable that I should be expected to live out there without an English maid. What would Aunt Margaret say?

'But — I can't do without a maid — an English one,' I said. 'I must have someone to dress my hair properly, and to see to my clothes.'

'The ayah is as good as any English maid. Besides, an English girl would not wish to go abroad and leave her family for an indefinite period — '

'Why not? I am,' I put in.

'That's different. You're getting married, and going out to your new home. You will have to get used to Indian servants, Adele.' There was a slight edge to Philip's voice.

As I sat there in the peace of the garden, with the spring flowers blooming everywhere, and the sound of birdcalls all around, I realized with a sense of shock that we were on the brink of a quarrel.

For the first time since I had met Philip, I felt quite nonplussed. It seemed wrong that he should oppose my taking an English maid with me. I felt that he should have understood that this was important to me, and that a young woman accompanying me from England would be a comfort when I found myself so far from home.

He sat looking straight in front of him. I darted him a timid glance, and saw that his handsome profile was set in hard lines. He was quite determined that I shouldn't take a maid from England . . . but I didn't want this ayah looking after me. I didn't care how good she was. Besides, *I* would be running the house when I got there, not the ayah.

These thoughts and many more passed through my mind as I sat there with Philip. It was all right saying I would have to get used to Indian servants. He had been brought up with them. But it wasn't the thought of

17

Indian servants in general which worried me. It was the thought of not having an English maid.

'Surely, Adele, if you regard an English maid as an essential you are very spoilt. And she would be as strange to the country as you, don't forget. How would she know how to deal with mosquitoes, for example? What it would really mean, is that the ayah would be looking after two of you, not one.'

On the face of it, most people would probably have thought that Philip was right. He knew better than I did what life was like in India. But surely, wanting an English maid didn't make me spoilt? Somewhat reluctantly, I agreed to drop the idea of getting one. Philip squeezed my hand, and said he knew that I was a sensible girl, but that I was too influenced by my aunt.

I was not sure if this statement was true or not. Certainly when I told Aunt Margaret that I was not taking a maid with me, she was absolutely confounded. Loyally I said that I agreed with Philip that it would not be necessary. But the grim expression on my aunt's face told me what she thought of the idea. And deep in my heart, although I would never have admitted it to her, I felt that she was right. But I was too much in love to make an issue of it. Besides, it would be still more of an adventure, going out to India without a maid.

As a result of this, I became less dependent on Eunice straight away. I found that I was quite capable of doing my hair myself, provided it was kept in a fairly simple style.

2

I had never thought very much about money. I just presumed that my aunt and uncle kept me in the same way that my parents would have done, had they lived. But now that I was to be married, Uncle Henry had a solicitor to the house, and in the library with them, I listened to a good deal of legal jargon about my position.

I learned, to my surprise, that I had money which was in trust until I was twenty one. If I married before that age, I came into my money then. I sat there in our comfortable library, with its big armchairs and many books, while Mr Faulkner and my uncle talked about my investments.

'What I really want to impress on my niece is that the money is *hers*,' said Uncle Henry ponderously. He looked across at Mr Faulkner, who adjusted his spectacles, and peered at me with his piercing grey eyes.

He cleared his throat. 'An Act has been very recently passed in Parliament, concerning a woman's money when she gets married. It's the Married Woman's Property Act, Miss Price. A husband now has no claim on his wife's money . . . '

His voice droned on. Uncle Henry opened a bottle of madeira and poured us out a glass each, while Mr Faulkner kept repeating how my money belonged to me and me alone.

I had two glasses of madeira, and felt rather between laughter and tears. 'It's such wonderful news, Uncle,' I said. 'And such a surprise, too.'

'We thought it better not to let you know you had expectations,' said my uncle. 'Your father and I were friends even before we married two girls from the same family. He was not a poor man by any means, my dear. He had a shrewd head on him, too, and I sometimes think you show signs of having one yourself.'

'Most unwise in many cases, to let a young girl know she has money to inherit,' put in Mr Faulkner. 'Very wise of you, Mr Barrett, to see the danger. Young people do not guard their tongues. And girls, being such guileless creatures — '

He shook his head, and sipped his madeira. I didn't really know what they meant by the 'danger'. But I was very pleased to know that I would have a comfortable income of my own. And how pleased Philip would be to hear it!

'Concerning the financial position of your husband-to-be,' went on Mr Faulkner, 'your uncle assures me that he has a prosperous business in India. We can only hope this is so.'

'As Adele's legal guardian, I have naturally worried a good deal as to whether I was making the right decision in allowing her to marry this young man,' said Uncle Henry, speaking rather as if I weren't there. 'The fact that she will have money of her own is both a blessing and an additional worry. But as you say, with the Married Woman's Property Act, she will be safeguarded.'

Later, when I told Philip about this, he seemed both pleased and surprised. I told him then what Mr Faulkner had said about the Married Woman's Property Act.

'I've never heard of that,' said Philip. I wanted him to be as amused about it all as much as I was, but he seemed rather quiet.

That evening we gave a dinner party. I wore a new gown of moiré silk, pale blue, with dark blue panels of velvet trimming the front. Eunice dressed my light brown hair in an elaborate style, and I felt pleased with my reflection as I sat in front of my dressing-table. Philip had said that he wanted us to be officially engaged, despite the fact that we were marrying so quickly, and now I wore a lovely solitaire diamond ring on the third finger of my left hand.

Both my aunt and uncle had been

suitably impressed, and of course, I had flashed it a great deal under Sophie's nose. I was fond of Sophie, but I knew that she had been rather surprised at the way Philip had pursued me; at first she had not believed he was in earnest. She had been impressed by him herself, and had called him handsome and charming the first evening he had danced with me.

Although she wished me every happiness for my future, I still felt that there was a tiny feeling of jealousy underneath. But then, what girl would not envy me? Sitting at our table, so pretty with the floral arrangement I had done, with Philip looking so handsome, and my diamond ring sparkling on my finger, I would not have changed places with anyone.

Excitedly I had told Sophie that I would come into money when I married. Rather to my chagrin, she was not surprised.

'I know. I've known for ages. Mama told me in confidence that your father had left money in trust for you.'

'Oh. I don't see why it should be regarded as a secret, anyway,' I said, rather annoyed that Sophie had known and I had not.

'Probably it's not as secret as all that,' she said, and dismissed the matter.

The dinner party was quite a gay affair, with much talk and laughter at the table. Afterwards, sitting in the drawing room with the other ladies, I hoped the gentlemen would not linger too long over their port and cigars, as I did not like to be parted from Philip. But they must have had much to discuss, because it was a long time before they joined us. When they did, I felt worried about Philip. He did not look well. His face had gone very pale, and his eyes had a strange expression in them.

'Is anything wrong?' I asked in a low voice. 'Are you ill, Philip?'

'Of course I'm not ill,' he muttered irritably. 'It's too hot in here, though. I'm going for a stroll round the gardens.'

The room was crowded; he left it abruptly. Most of the guests were busily engaged in conversation, or playing cards, but Uncle Henry seemed to have witnessed my discomfiture.

'What is wrong, Adele?' he asked, in a quick aside.

'I'm worried about Philip,' I said. 'I'm sure he's not well — you must have noticed when you were in the dining room. He says he's going for a walk in the garden.'

My uncle looked embarrassed. 'He should not have come into the drawing room,' he said. 'I doubt if you will see him again tonight, Adele, and it's perhaps just as well that you shouldn't.'

'Why not?' I asked indignantly, although still in a low voice. 'If he is feeling ill, I should try to help him.'

Uncle Henry looked as if he didn't know what to say.

'My dear, please help your aunt to entertain the other guests,' he said at last. 'I myself will go and ascertain that Philip is all right. But pray, do not mention anything to the rest of the company. We don't want any gossip.'

I did not understand what he meant. I was still concerned about Philip, but I felt easier in my mind when I saw my uncle discreetly leave the drawing room. Some of the company were staying the night at Onger House; others would be leaving at a later hour. My uncle did not return for some time, and I hid my anxiety as best I could. When he finally reappeared, he said that Philip begged to be excused joining the rest of the company, as he was feeling somewhat unwell.

'He has gone to his room,' he told me in private.

The rest of the evening went off smoothly, but I did not enjoy it. Nor did I sleep well, for wondering how Philip was. I was down for breakfast with Sophie, but although some of the guests were assembled, Philip was not among them.

'If you ask me — ' began Sophie, as she helped herself to kidneys — 'I think the gentlemen must have drunk too many toasts!'

'Perhaps so — something must have upset Philip,' I said anxiously. I felt like going to his room, but I knew that would not be regarded as seemly. Uncle Henry sensed that I was worried, and told me there was no cause for concern; Philip had a headache and was spending the morning in bed.

Fortunately there was much to do, with some guests still in the house, and I had no time for brooding. At luncheon, to my joy, Philip appeared, looking somewhat pale. He told me in private that he was sorry he'd had to leave the company the night before; it was merely a stomach upset, and he would soon be well.

'But you should take something for it — you don't *look* well — ' I began.

'I shall be all right. Don't *fuss* so, Adele,' he said, with more than a touch of irritation in his voice.

We were about to take our places at table. It was a cold luncheon, after the splendours of the dinner party the night before. To my surprise, I saw my uncle carefully mixing a drink; he had sent to the kitchen for some of the ingredients.

'The best thing in the world for you, Philip,' he said, with a kindly smile, and handed it to my fiancé.

With a rather wry face, Philip drank it, to the accompaniment of a certain amount of chaffing from the other men. I was still somewhat in the dark about the whole thing; not so Sophie, apparently. She was more worldly wise than I, perhaps due to the fact that she lived in London.

'I told you! Too many toasts,' she said, smiling. 'You are green, Adele.'

When I realized what she meant, I felt indignant with the other men for making him drink too much. However, later in the day he seemed to revive, and the incident did not appear important. Much more important were the plans for our honeymoon, which we decided to spend in North Wales. But before that was the wedding.

★ ★ ★

I could hear the patter of rain on the hotel bedroom window. If I drew back the curtains I would see grey rain-clouds half covering the mountains. We were having very mixed weather on our honeymoon.

Philip was huddled under the bed-clothes, still asleep. I lay thinking of my wedding day. The sun had shone, and the village church had been crowded. My gown was of white taffeta, and I carried a bouquet of red roses, fresh from our own garden. Sophie and a girl I had been friendly with from child-hood were my bridesmaids, both in blue.

Uncle Henry looked extremely solemn as he escorted me down the aisle; I knew that Aunt Margaret was in tears. Twice she had needed smelling salts, the morning of the wedding. Philip looked exceedingly handsome, like a hero from a novel. At the altar he gave my hand a reassuring squeeze. I found it hard to believe that I could be the cause of making a man like him happy.

It was all a bit dreamlike, looking back to such a short time ago. The kisses, the tears, the champagne, and all the good wishes. There was an unexpected ache in my heart when we left to go on our honeymoon. Eunice had cried openly as she helped me change into my new grey travelling costume. There had been some talk of her accompanying me to Wales, but Philip had said it wasn't really necessary.

'If you can manage your own hair, I can act as lady's maid,' he said lightly.

I could feel myself blushing slightly at the prospect. Rather to my surprise, though, I found that Philip coped competently with hooks and eyes, and like things, and I managed very well. In any case, I had been trying to be independent of Eunice as much as possible, in view of the fact that I was going to do without a maid altogether.

I looked at my new, gold wedding ring gleaming on my finger, as I lay in bed. Mrs Belvedere! I still found it hard to believe. And soon, thousands of miles away in India, in a house called Lebanon, they would be making preparations for Philip's return — with his bride.

There was only one tiny thing which seemed to flaw my happiness. It was something which I could not bring myself to mention to Philip; something, indeed, which was difficult for me to understand. My husband appeared to drink more freely than I had realized, and yet, I felt I should not comment on this, because, after all, we were on our honeymoon. Apart from that, I really had little idea how much it was normal for a man to drink.

I knew my uncle drank wine, and brandy as well, but never very much at a time. Philip drank quite a lot at luncheon every day, and again in the evenings. And yet, was this unusual for a man on honeymoon? After all, it was a special occasion in his life, was I worrying unduly over things? Once we were settled in Sadura he would have plenty to do.

After all, he'd had several months holiday in England, and no doubt was tiring of his inactive life . . .

He woke, and reached out his arm, smiling in the half light of the morning. 'I've been dreaming, Adele,' he murmured sleepily. 'I've been dreaming I was back in India.'

'Well, you soon will be,' I whispered. 'With me.'

'Yes . . . ' he paused, his black eyebrows drawing together in a frown. 'Dearest, there is something I want to talk over with you. Of course, this is in confidence, as husband and wife.'

'Of course,' I echoed, a little surprised. 'Is it something important?'

'In a way it is, dear. It's about money.'

'Yes?'

'As you know, I've had to face quite a lot of expense in England — unexpected expense. Naturally, I don't begrudge a penny of all I've spent. It means that just now, though — well, funds are running rather low. It's rather embarrassing to have to discuss this with you, but I wonder if you would lend me some money before we leave for India? I hate having to ask you like this, but these are rather exceptional circumstances.'

'Why, of course,' I said. 'Marriage is sharing, isn't it?'

'You are sweet, Adele,' murmured Philip, kissing my hair. 'I don't know what I've done to deserve you.'

That was exactly how I felt towards him.

'It's a pity that your capital has to remain in England,' he went on. 'However, there seems to be nothing we can do about that.'

'Uncle Henry seems quite pleased about that,' I replied. 'He says people don't touch capital; anyway, it's mostly in investments — I don't know much about it. But he says my income from the capital will be in a bank in Madras.'

'Yes, your income will be available,' said Philip. 'It's funny that you never knew you had money to come to you on marriage.'

'I never gave things like that much thought,' I said. 'I had an allowance from Uncle, and all the clothes I needed. So I never really had much need to think about money. I like the idea of having money of my own — money which my father left me. Although now, of course, it is ours.'

Philip gave me a squeeze. 'If it hadn't been for this new-fangled Married Woman's Property Act, it would all have been mine now, anyway.'

'Uncle kept talking about that Act. As if Acts of Parliament have anything to do with people in love!'

'Still, I suppose money is something which two people have to think about after marriage,' said Philip lightly. 'I'm like you — I've never thought it really very important. It's just unfortunate that I've overspent recently. When our honeymoon here is over, we'll take a trip to London. You can say you're going to do some last minute shopping

35

before we sail for India, and we can visit your bank while we are staying in London.'

'Oh, yes! We could stay at Sophie's — '

'Adele, dearest, I do not wish to stay at your Aunt Mary's. We'll stay at an hotel. And don't mention at home that you intend to visit your bank. What you do from now on has nothing to do with your aunt and uncle. You are a married woman.'

He kissed me, as if to emphasize the point.

'I'm still getting used to the idea,' I said. I had never in my life gone to London and not stayed at Aunt Mary's, but then I had never gone as a married woman before. But as for my affairs being nothing to do with my aunt and uncle, somehow I felt Philip was not being quite fair to them. I knew that they fussed over me to the point of irritation, and wanted to know all sorts of things, but I still knew that I was lucky to have them. They had taken the place of my parents, and fulfilled their responsibilities towards me, but they had given me love, too.

'Penny for your thoughts,' said Philip.

'Oh . . . just thinking. No, I won't tell Aunt Margaret anything about our money situation. But in any case, there's nothing odd about one drawing money out of a bank.'

'I never said there was, dearest. Only I would prefer you to keep our affairs private. It's just a matter of transferring some of your money to my account.'

'How much had you in mind?'

'Well, let me see, dear. All things considered, I think perhaps you had better make it a thousand pounds.'

'A thousand pounds!' I gasped. 'But that's a lot of money, surely. I didn't really think you meant as much as that.'

'Good gracious, Adele, what a child you are! Do you really think a thousand pounds is a lot of money? Why, it's nothing these days.'

I lay without speaking, thinking about it. It was true that I had never thought particularly about the value of money, because I had never really had cause to, up to the time of my marriage. No doubt Philip was right about that, but it still seemed a lot of money to me, and I said so again.

My husband made an impatient sound, and drew his arm away pettishly. 'I'm afraid, Adele, you have a lot to learn about the world. When I came to England, naturally, I didn't know I was going to meet you, and face all the expense which I've had to. If you're making a fuss straight away about a thousand pounds, it doesn't sound much like marriage being for sharing from your point of view.'

'Philip — darling! Don't be silly. Of course I'll draw it out. Don't let's quarrel, please.'

We made it up after that, and later that day the sun came out, and we had a happy time together. The loveliness and majesty of the scenery made me realize with a little pang that I would soon be exchanging all that for an unknown land.

But that was what I wanted — a challenge from life. I told Aunt Margaret so, shortly before my departure.

'A challenge from life?' she repeated. 'You'll have that all right, Adele. That's something we all get — and you don't have to go to India for it, either. But still, you're not penniless, and if you are not happy there, don't stay. I'm sure if Philip realizes you are not settling, he will bring you back, and settle in England with you. Do remember, never go out in that sun unless you are properly protected from it, or your skin will be ruined.'

'Aunt Margaret, don't worry so much about these things. After all, Philip knows all about living out there — surely he will look after me.'

'I sincerely hope he will, my dear. And I hope he will bring you back if you are not happy.'

I made no reply to this. For one thing, my aunt was a bit like a steamroller when she started on a subject, particularly if it was anything to do with my going to India. For another thing, there was something about Philip which she didn't realize, and which I was only just beginning to realize myself.

India was home to him, not England. Like all colonials, he called England home, but it was just a word.

'It's been wonderful, coming home, meeting you, our wedding, our honeymoon, everything,' he had said on our last day in Wales. I stood beside him without speaking, and we gazed at the sunlit view of streams and mountains. For a moment I had a terrible pang of sadness.

'I shall miss all this,' I said. 'Won't you?'

'Not really. I'll have you beside me on the verandah at Lebanon, and we'll watch the sun sink into the sea every night. And we'll hear the squirrels pattering around in the darkness . . . '

There was a queer sort of excitement in his voice. And I knew then how much he wanted to get back to India.

3

I sat alone in the drawing room at Lebanon, writing a letter to Aunt Margaret. It would take such a long time for it to reach England.

England . . . I thought of that interminable voyage to India. I could not believe it when we stepped off the boat at last. The journey to Sadura had been tiring enough afterwards, too. The heat was not too bad at the moment; indeed, this was supposed to be about the best time of the year, according to Philip.

I glanced round the room. It was charming, with a large couch, and comfortable chairs. There was a good deal of beautiful, carved woodwork, and the floor was covered in polished tiles from the factory. There were several lovely china vases and figurines, and the walls of both the drawing room and the dining room as well as the pillars of the verandah were finished to look like porcelain. It was not porcelain, though, but egg-shell *chunam*, an art which Philip had told me was gradually dying out.

The room seemed dominated by a portrait of a dark-haired, very beautiful girl in a pink and gold ball dress of a bygone fashion. It was Philip's French mother, Leone.

Below the house, the delightful garden fell away to the creek that ran between well-tended banks, and the factory lay down the creek and round a corner. You could not see a trace of it from Lebanon, although Philip had told me you could smell the kilns from the house during the monsoon.

It was very pleasant, I wrote to Aunt Margaret. I was settling down in Sadura. Settling down . . . well, what else could I tell her? I couldn't tell her about some things — I simply couldn't!

I heard a movement outside the verandah, and then footsteps in the

42

house. *Her* footsteps; shuff-shuff, shuff-shuff, on the tiles.

The ayah. She would be outside the drawing room door now. She knew I was in there, just as she knew everything. Everything that went on in Lebanon; everything that went on in Sadura. I could picture her outside the door now, in her dark blue sari, with her great, heavy earrings swinging from her ears. Her hair was blue-black, just touched with grey at her temples, her skin was dark olive, and her eyes were dark, and inscrutable too. I suppose in her youth she must have been a striking woman, because she was tall and majestic, and she carried herself well.

She always wore slippers with turned-up toes in the house. I seemed to be forever listening for the sound they made on the tiled floor, shuff-shuff, shuff-shuff. Her name was Urmilla, but she was never called by it. She was always 'the ayah'; when Philip addressed her, he called her 'Ayah'. And she was here to stay.

I longed to start that letter to Aunt Margaret all over again, and tell her there were things I neither liked nor understood about Lebanon. For one thing, with the exception of the ayah, and Babwah, the houseboy, the servants didn't bother to speak English much in the house. They spoke an Indian dialect language, Telugu, and this is what I heard around me most of the day. Philip spoke it too, spoke it with apparently as much ease as he spoke English.

Somehow I hadn't imagined any language but English being spoken in the house, but when I said so, he seemed much amused.

'It's natural for them to speak in Telugu to each other.' When they did speak English, they spoke in a sing-song kind of way, not unlike the people in North Wales, where we had honeymooned.

The ayah had a queer little bungalow beyond the creek, in another part of the garden. I was thankful she didn't live on the premises. The other servants had their own huts at the back of the house, except for Babwah, the houseboy, who always slept in the kitchen. He was not the only houseboy, and strictly speaking, he was no longer a boy, but I liked Babwah, although I always felt he was afraid of the ayah.

I was glad that I was used to managing without a maid. I had done my hair myself on the voyage from England, and I had become quite expert at it. Occasionally I had to ask Philip's assistance when dressing, but on the whole I had become virtually independent of anyone.

At first, the ayah took it for granted she would be acting as maid to me. On my first day at Lebanon, she appeared in the bedroom, and, kneeling down, slipped off my shoes and stockings. Then she began to rub something into my legs.

'What is she doing?' I cried, embarrassed, to Philip.

'I expect she's rubbing you with

citronella oil to keep away the mosquitoes,' he replied.

Right from first meeting her, I had this peculiar aversion, this curious feeling of mistrust for the ayah. Her voice was polite when she spoke to me, her face was expressionless, but I somehow knew instinctively that she didn't want me at Lebanon.

I made it plain that I had no need of her services as lady's maid. I would rub my legs myself with citronella oil, if need be. I resented the way she had the run of the house; the way she ordered the other servants around. And yet, there was nothing that I could really complain about. Philip had remarked that if there was any sort of crisis in the home while he was at the tile factory, he was glad the ayah was there to deal with things.

Shuff-shuff, shuff-shuff; the footsteps passed on. Philip and I were giving a dinner party that evening, the first since we had arrived from England. I had carefully written out the invitations in my best copperplate hand-writing, asking Philip details of the people we were inviting, not all of whom I had met.

'Who's Dr Baxter?' I asked.

'He's a widower. His wife died a couple of years ago — not long after they came to Sadura.'

'He'll be an older man, then.'

'No, he's not much over thirty, I believe. They hadn't been married very long.'

'And Mr and Mrs Snow?'

'They are older people. He's a retired engineer. They were friendly with my parents years ago. They're a very old established couple here.'

One by one the invitations were written out and commented on. The guests were mostly planters and their wives; a sprinkling of Civil Servants and the doctor made up the list. I was pleased that we were beginning to have some social life, because I was eager to feel more settled in Sadura. It had taken me about a month to get used to being on board ship; by the time we had arrived in India, I felt as though I had been on a boat for half my life.

The voyage had not been an unqualified success, as I had not proved the best of sailors. Although Philip had been kind and attentive for the most part, there were times when his patience had worn thin. On more than one occasion he had left me in the cabin, and spent the evening with some other passengers.

I remember dozing off once in a kind of sick daze, and waking to see him come back to the cabin. It was very late. I asked him what he had been doing, and he replied that he had been playing cards. I suspected that he had been drinking quite heavily, too. Under the influence of the sedative which the doctor had given me, I felt too tired to question him further. In the morning, when I felt a bit better, he was so charming and attentive that I decided not to say anything about it.

Nevertheless, this was something

which worried me, something which I would think about, and then push to the back of my mind. There was nothing wrong with a man having a drink. I had heard my uncle say that many a time. I knew that it was true, of course, and yet there were times when I was sure Philip drank too much. He drank spirits as well as wine. In the evenings, when we sat on the verandah together, he drank brandy. I never said anything about this, because I really didn't know what to say, or how to put things. Besides, I knew by now that Philip had a way of ridiculing me if I made a remark which he thought was stupid. This made me rather careful before I ventured on an opinion. He was several years older than I, and I knew that he considered I had led a very sheltered life, and that my aunt and uncle were an old-fashioned pair.

So I held my peace about one or two things at Lebanon. After all, it was early days — and I didn't want to start finding fault with Philip, or my new home, or anything.

I dressed carefully for our dinner party that evening, with my husband's assistance. I knew that he thought I should let the ayah help me; probably my hair was not as elaborately dressed as it should have been, but that was one point which I was being obstinate on. My flounced white dress looked very cool and pretty, though. Philip dropped a kiss on the nape of my neck.

'I want to show you off,' he murmured. 'I want to show them all at Sadura what I've brought back from home.'

Fortunately, we had a very good cook at Lebanon. His name was Samsoodeen, usually shortened to Sam. All the meals were well cooked and served; I had nothing to complain of in that respect. The same dishes seemed to appear over and over again, though. Apparently there was nothing to be done about this; Sam would not have taken kindly to any new ideas.

'Sam has been the cook here for

years, Adele, and he's a very good cook. Besides, he cooks what I like. I don't want the meals changing — after all, he's well used to my tastes.'

This was something which I could not dispute. I simply had no grounds for trying to change the menus — my husband liked things the way they were. So here again I felt oddly frustrated, and yet there was nothing I could do. Apart from that, I had little knowledge of cooking, anyway. It was not as though I could show Sam myself what I wanted doing.

In the dining room a white cloth had covered the shining rosewood table, in the centre of which was a bowl of floating temple flowers. The silver, the napery, the glasses — yes, it all looked very nice.

Philip had told me that quite a number of the men played cricket, which I thought was probably a good idea, even though it must get uncomfortably hot at times. Bullock-coaches were now driving up, and our guests

51

were arriving. I felt quite excited. I stood with my husband on the great verandah at Lebanon, and welcomed them.

I was well aware that I was receiving plenty of glances from my new neighbours as the introductions were performed. There was only one other really young couple, the Radstocks, who were in their twenties. The rest appeared to be over thirty; a few of the couples were quite middle-aged, including the Snows.

Pre-dinner drinks were served, or *chota-pegs,* as I was learning to call them.

'And how do you think you are going to like living in Sadura, Mrs Belvedere?' enquired Mr Radstock, kindly. He was in the Indian Civil Service; a slight, fair young man, with rather a nervous manner. His wife, Judith, was plump and dark.

'I'm sure I shall like it,' I replied. 'It is all rather strange at present, of course.'

'Which part of England do you come

from?' asked his wife. I was showered with questions from first one and then the other. I was a little surprised to find that more than one of our guests had been born in India, and had lived there ever since, without once visiting England. And yet they called it 'home' like everyone else. But it was no more home to them than it was to Philip.

We took our places at the dinner table, where Babwah and the ayah waited on us.

Asparagus, olives, fish with tomato-rice, rounds of mutton sitting on slices of orange, turkey with ham and sausage and bread sauce, toffee-basket pudding, drunk prunes — it was certainly a substantial meal, and the guests did full justice to it.

I was sitting next to Dr Baxter. He was a tall, and, I thought at first, slightly withdrawn man. He had fair hair, and a very pleasant smile. His eyes were sad, though, and I remembered Philip saying that he had lost his young wife.

'You must be everyone's doctor, then,

I suppose?' I said rather nervously.

He smiled then. 'Yes. And yours if necessary, I have no doubt.'

'If necessary,' I said, smiling too. 'I do not ail much, I am happy to say.'

'Did you ail on the crossing?' he asked, a little slyly.

'Oh, well, a bit,' I admitted.

'But you are well now. And the heat hasn't robbed you of your English rose complexion yet.'

I found myself blushing unexpectedly.

'It is a big thing — I mean, to leave England and your family, and make a home in a strange land. You would only know your husband a short time before you married him.'

'Yes,' I said happily. 'I had to make up my mind quickly — and I did. Everyone said it was too big a decision to make, and all the rest of it, and my aunt and uncle were not happy about my coming to India. But I wanted a challenge from life — I told my aunt so.'

I was a little vexed with myself for having told a stranger so much in such a short time, but Dr Baxter did not appear surprised.

'I think you will find all the challenge you want at Sadura,' he said quietly, and this time he did not smile. For a moment I wondered what he meant, but he changed the subject quickly, and asked me if I did not think Lebanon a charming house, set in such a lovely garden, with great, towering cedar trees surrounding it.

He did not monopolize the conversation, though. A good many topics were discussed at dinner, and the men were beginning to talk about cricket by the time the dessert arrived. The ayah waited at table very well; smoothly, silently, she removed plates and brought fresh ones. Shuff-shuff, shuff-shuff, in and out of the room, never obtrusive, always there when she was required.

I saw that it was time to lead the ladies into the drawing room, and leave the men to discuss cricket, or whatever it was they were bent on discussing when alone.

'How do you get on with the ayah?' enquired Mrs Walker. She was a thin, dark, middle-aged woman, persistently fanning herself with a beautiful ivory fan. Was it my imagination, or did everyone in the room suddenly seem to become silent, waiting for my reply?

'The ayah?' I repeated brightly. 'Well, I suppose she's more or less an institution here, isn't she?'

'Yes,' said Mrs Snow. 'So many things here are institutions. I believe the Telugu word is *mamul,* the law. I suppose you've seen all round the factory by now?' She was a large, plump person, and I liked her straight away.

'No,' I said. 'I'll have to get Philip to take me round one day. There are so many things to see, and so many things to do all at once, that it's impossible to do everything.'

'So *many* things to see,' repeated Mrs Walker slowly.

I had a sudden, rather unpleasant

feeling that there was a significance behind her remark, but I could just as well have been mistaken.

'It's five years since I saw England,' remarked Mrs Radstock rather wistfully. 'Tell me how London was looking last time you saw it. I'm sure our fashions are a long way behind out here.'

'Not really,' I said politely. I was merely being kind, though, because there was no doubt about it, all the ladies had a slightly old-fashioned look about them. Clearly, nobody could be quite as stylish here as back home. I told them about London, and the shows which I had seen with Philip, and the shops, and all the other things which they seemed interested in.

'Life goes on with such a sameness at Sadura,' remarked one of the ladies in a discontented voice.

'It probably seems like that, wherever you live,' said Mrs Walker. 'Plenty of things happen here. My goodness, when I think of some of the things

. . . Dr Baxter coming out here to practice in this backwater, bringing his young wife with him. And then he lost her after they had only been married about three years! Poor boy, I don't know how he carried on the way he did. And then there was the business of the Forrester girl — '

'The gentlemen are lingering together, aren't they?' broke in Mrs Snow in a brisk voice.

'I often wonder what they talk about when they are all together,' remarked Mrs Walker. She seemed on the point of saying more, but the men arrived at that moment, all talking at once, or so it sounded to us. How handsome Philip looked, I thought. He was certainly the best looking man there. I felt a little glow of pride, and relief, too. I had not forgotten that upsetting evening at Onger House when he had not been well.

Dr Baxter was looking at me. What kind blue eyes he had. He was not handsome like Philip, but he had a nice face, a strong chin, and a charming smile.

'Our hostess must have been thinking we were never going to put in an appearance,' he said. 'I'm afraid we've been discussing everything from cabbages to kings.'

'So have we,' said Mrs Walker, who was seldom quiet for long. 'We've been talking about everything — London fashions, and how nothing happens in Sadura, but everything happens really, and how Mrs Belvedere is settling down — and heavens, how many years has the ayah been on the go?'

I was sure that there was an almost imperceptible silence again; a curious sort of embarrassment in the assembled company.

'Ever since anyone can remember, I should think,' said her husband, rather shortly, it seemed to me.

We had a pleasant evening. The talk was about all sorts of things; people exchanged anecdotes, asked questions about England; invited me to one or two social functions with Philip. The planters discussed business occasionally, and compared notes. All the time I had the feeling that I was being sized up by the women; by the men, too, but not in quite the same way.

'You haven't really known my husband very long, have you?' I asked Dr Baxter. We were being served coffee now by the ayah; soon the bullock-coaches would depart with the guests.

'Not really. I came out here about three years ago to practice in Sadura. I felt I could fulfil a greater need in a place like this than back home. My father has a country practice in Gloucestershire — I hear you are from the West Country, too.'

'Yes — from Wiltshire. The ladies were saying how nothing happens in Sadura, and yet, everything happens.'

'How true!'

'I suppose I like things to happen,' I said. 'It's more exciting.'

'Sometimes. Not always.' His face took on a closed-in look. I realized I had touched on past sadness in his life.

I changed the subject hastily, and the talk became more general.

Later, I stood with my husband and waved off the departing company. Out on the verandah it was starlit, silent save for the faint squeaks and scuffles of squirrels. Philip slipped his arm round my waist, and for a few minutes we stood without speaking. I remembered how he had talked about this when we were on our honeymoon, and how eager he had been to get back to Sadura.

The evening had gone very well; I had the promise of new friends, and a reasonable social life. But somehow I felt that there was something wrong. I couldn't put it into words. My husband kissed me, a lingering kiss before we went inside. It reassured me; there was nothing wrong, it was just a passing feeling of depression.

Probably it was the strangeness of everything, and being so far away from England. The house was silent; the ayah had gone. Hand in hand we went upstairs and into the bedroom.

4

I sat in front of my rosewood dressing-table, and made a leisurely toilette before ordering the bullock-coach to take me to Mrs Radstock's for a morning visit. Apparently her husband was in Madras on business matters for a week or so, and she had asked some of her friends round for a ladies only tiffin.

When I had mentioned this to Philip, he said that he thought it would be a good idea for me to go, as he had business too, in a place called Hush Hush Valley.

'Business?' I had asked, in some surprise. 'What sort of business?'

'Oh . . . connected with coffee.' He seemed to hesitate before telling me.

'I didn't know you had anything to do with coffee.'

'It's not much, really. Just a coffee-garden. I shall have to visit it from time to time. Don't mention where I have gone, though. when you go out to tiffin. People are so inclined to gossip here. If you are in business, they want to know too much about it. I realize it's hard for you to understand all this, darling. It's very nice for you to have friends, but I don't wish you to discuss any of our affairs with them — the tile factory, or the coffee-garden, or any thing. You won't, will you?'

'Not if you don't wish it,' I said slowly, somewhat mystified. I thought then, not for the first time, that there was a curiously secretive streak in my husband. Why shouldn't I mention the coffee-garden at Hush Hush Valley?

Philip dropped a quick kiss on the nape of my neck. 'I'll be back tomorrow evening.'

I thought about his rather baffling attitude as I sat in the bedroom with its large, ornate furniture and long mirrors. The strange unease which I was constantly experiencing, and just as constantly ignoring, seemed to come back again. We had been by train to Madras so that I could collect my allowance about a fortnight before. In a roundabout sort of way, Philip had asked me for some money afterwards.

'It's just to help the tile factory along. Sometimes it goes through bad patches — nothing serious, you understand.'

I gave him the money, but there were things which I didn't understand. I wanted him to take me round the tile factory, but he refused to do so. He said it was no place for me; that there were natives working there, and that it wasn't very pleasant.

'Anyway, what would you want worrying your head about the tile factory?'

As I sat in the bedroom that morning, I turned this over in my mind. I didn't like all this secrecy. It was *our* tile factory after all. Besides, another thought kept coming into my mind. Philip seemed quite prepared to take money from me to use in the factory. I didn't mind this, it was *our* money, but

I wanted to go round the factory and see things for myself. Then I might understand my husband if he wanted to talk about it. I might even be able to make some useful suggestions. Philip sometimes laughed at me teasingly because he thought I was not very worldly wise, but that was the way he seemed to want to keep me. Surely in this day and age, whatever was a husband's business was his wife's business as well?

I put on a bonnet and veil, picked up a parasol, and prepared to leave the bedroom. As I descended the stairs I heard the shuff-shuff of the ayah's feet going into the kitchen. How much did *she* know of our business, I wondered. I had any uneasy feeling that she knew a great deal — probably more than I did. It was all very unsatisfactory.

The bullock-coach driver, Ramdeen, spoke English quite well. It was a pleasant drive along the red, laterite road to the Radstocks' bungalow. On the way I passed Dr Baxter's place, set well back from the road, but still very accessible should anyone need his services in a hurry. I thought about him coming to India because he thought his services would be of more value here than in England. I had been told that his wife had gone into a decline, and there was nothing anyone could do to save her. I reflected that in his position, I should have wanted to leave Sadura and its unhappy memories behind, not stayed on as he had.

I was beginning to feel less of a stranger in this country already. During the train journey to Madras and back, I had absorbed the newness of the scenery, so different from what I was used to in Wiltshire. This was a land of green paddy fields, red laterite hills, and little villages. There were rivers with palm trees on the banks, and intriguing, half-hidden temples dotted here and there. It was beautiful, mysterious, foreign, and yet, my eyes were growing used to it.

Mrs Radstock greeted me pleasantly

on the verandah of her bungalow. Some of the ladies were already present. In the drawing room we were served with cool drinks, and the main conversation seemed to be about Christmas, which was now quite close.

It seemed strange to me that we would eat turkey and plum pudding without the least prospect of snow. Somehow it did not seem like Christmas, but from what everyone was saying, it was celebrated in the usual way, except that it was warm weather.

'Are you feeling less strange here now?' enquired Mrs Walker.

'Yes, I think I'm settling down more,' I replied.

'And what is your husband doing today?' she went on, wielding her inevitable fan. I noticed then what sharp eyes she had, unpleasantly penetrating.

'Busy, as usual,' I said lightly.

'I saw him going out of the town in the direction of the Ghat road. On his way somewhere, I suppose.' She raised her eyebrows questioningly, but I did not take her up on that. I decided there and then that Mrs Walker could be something of a mischief-maker.

'There's one thing about living here, as you'll find out,' she went on with rather a forced laugh. 'There's precious little the servants don't know about what goes on. They know everything that goes on in that native bazaar — everything. In fact they know what we're going to do before we know ourselves. Isn't that a fact, ladies? I remember, that to-do with poor Dorothy Forrester — '

She shook her head. I remembered, then. She had mentioned the name Forrester before, and the others had changed the subject. Determinedly I smiled, and did not encourage her to pursue any of the subjects at which she was half hinting. On the whole, the ladies seemed friendly, and kindly disposed towards me. I particularly liked Mrs Radstock. She was young and cheerful, and tried to make me feel at home in her bungalow that day.

I liked Mrs Snow, too. She was motherly, and I felt that in her I had a friend I could turn to if the need arose. During tiffin, which was nicely cooked and served, I found myself thinking this, and then immediately wondered why. As I had told my uncle when I wanted to marry Philip, how could I be alone or in need of friends when I had my husband?

I was still the main attraction among the wives at Sadura. They one and all seemed interested in me. True, I was the most recent arrival from England, but that was only part of the interest I seemed to arouse. I had an uneasy feeling that the fact that I had married Philip Belvedere was a source of some gossip. When he had said he wanted to show me off to everyone, was it just the normal pride of a bridegroom, or was it something deeper?

'You look serious, Mrs Belvedere. Are you feeling quite well?' My hostess looked at me with kind, anxious brown eyes.

I laughed. 'Yes, of course. I was thinking how nice this curry is.'

'If you have a good cook in the home, it makes up for a lot,' remarked Mrs Snow. 'I rarely go into my kitchen — it's full of that foul beedi they smoke. But there, Singh cooks reasonably well, so we must just be grateful. Your cook has been with the family for years, Mrs Belvedere.'

'So I understand,' I said.

'If you have a good staff of servants, hang on to them by all means — like grim death,' remarked Mrs Walker, attacking her curry with vigour. 'We had your ayah's brother on our household staff for a while, and he was no asset. He was drunk on that frightful cashew-arrack for most of the time. The rest of it he devoted to his devil-dancing, or whatever it is.'

'Devil-dancing?' A sudden cold chill struck through me.

'He's a horrible old man,' put in Mrs Snow quickly. 'He's a lot older than the ayah. My husband saw him once, all done up, with his face stained with yellow ochre, and coconut leaves round his head. The tom-toms were beating, and he was leaping around like one possessed, shouting at the top of his voice. He's supposed to have magic powers and all the rest of it.'

Somehow I had never imagined the ayah having a brother. This was news to me. Philip had told me that she had been widowed when quite young.

'I'm thankful he doesn't live with the ayah, then,' I said.

'She lives alone now, doesn't she?' said Mrs Walker.

The subject was changed, then, and I was left wondering. On the whole, though, I enjoyed the company, and the tiffin. As I set off back in the bullock-coach I wondered if I was just imagining things about the attitude of the ladies of Sadura; about the ayah, and about a host of other things.

It was late afternoon when I arrived back at Lebanon. I dined alone, and spent most of the evening writing letters. I did not care to be left alone like this, but Philip had explained that the journey to Hush Hush Valley took quite a while, and he could not get back the same day. I was pleased to see him when he did return the following day. I was sitting on the verandah waiting for him.

How nice he looked in his wide-brimmed Terai hat. He removed it and bent to kiss me.

'Did you enjoy yourself yesterday, dear?' he asked.

'Yes. It was very pleasant indeed. Did you?'

He gave a slightly rueful smile, 'I went on business, not pleasure.'

'But all is well at the coffee-garden?' I persisted, as we entered the house together.

'Er — yes. As well as ever.'

'Who runs the place?' I went on.

'You are a curious little thing, aren't you? I simply can't understand why you are so interested in the tile factory and the coffee plantation. It's run by an

Indian, if you must know.'

We had dinner together, after which Philip sat smoking a cheroot and drinking brandy.

'Mrs Walker said the ayah's brother used to be one of their house servants, and that he was hopeless, and always half drunk. She says he's a devil-dancer, whatever that is.'

Philip raised his dark eyebrows. 'Gossip, gossip — I warned you how the good ladies of Sadura talk. Of course there are bad servants here, the same as in England. And of course quite a lot of them drink — and they have their devil-dancers, and all the rest of it. And why not?'

He poured out another large brandy, and sat drinking it with a rather sullen expression on his face.

When I had given him some money after visiting Madras, he had talked vaguely of 'cutting down on expenses'. I remembered how he had played cards on the voyage to India, and I was pretty sure he had played

73

for money. If he wanted to cut down on expenses, I saw no sign of him doing so. Not for the first time I thought the ayah could go, and I would shed no tears. I was an active and capable girl; if the ayah left I would have more to do in the way of dealing with the other servants.

'When we came back from Madras, you were talking of cutting down on expenses,' I began, rather nervously.

'Well?' He looked still more sullen.

'I can think of a number of ways to do that,' I said cheerfully. 'I've been thinking how lucky we are with our servants, really.'

The response was a non-committal grunt.

'The fact that the household seems to run so smoothly and that we have a good cook makes me think that we don't really need the ayah here at all — ' I broke off at the look of anger on his face.

'The ayah stays.'

For a moment I was silent, then I

burst out with 'Why? I don't need her as a maid — I don't need her at all — '

'Whatever you need or don't need,' he repeated, 'the ayah stays.'

Anger and bewilderment struggled inside me. The truculent expression on his face; the brandy he was drinking so freely, and above all, his seeming disregard for my wishes, brought all my hidden fears to the surface.

'Why should she stay?' I cried, my cheeks burning with anger. 'This is my home as well as yours — mine! You talked about us sharing everything when we were on honeymoon — you mean you want to share everything that is mine! It's a different story as soon as I want to do anything my way. You try to keep me out of everything — you try to keep me from seeing the factory — '

I was pulled up short by Philip seizing my wrists in a tight grip. 'You're getting hysterical,' he said scornfully. 'You need the ayah to give you a soothing draft, or something. Come on upstairs, you've had a tiring time

75

listening to a lot of gossip while I've been away.'

Holding me firmly, he led me up the stairs to our large bedroom with the adjoining dressing room. I was so frightened by his manner that I was speechless; I was panting with a mixture of fear and anger. We entered the bedroom, and he pushed me down roughly on the bed.

'Now you can stay here and cool down. Otherwise, I shall get the ayah to make up a good native brew that will keep you quiet for several hours.' He left the room, closing the door behind him.

For a few minutes I lay on the bed sobbing, unable to believe that the ugly scene which had taken place could really have happened. I was shocked to my innermost being. Could this be the same man who had pursued me with such tender ardour in England, only a few short months before? He had been so loving, so attentive, why had he changed like this? Why had he become so enraged when I had suggested we didn't need the ayah? Why? Why?

When my sobs subsided, I lay there for a long time. There was no sound anywhere; the house was silent. An hour passed; two hours. At last I undressed slowly, by the light of the oil lamp. When I looked at myself in the mirror I seemed to be looking at a stranger; a girl with her hair in a long plait, a girl with big, frightened eyes.

It would blow over, I told myself. He would come to bed soon. I mustn't get too upset; it was only a tiff. Surely all married couples must have them sometimes. I was shivering, but hot at the same time. Lying on the bed, under the mosquito net, I relived my life from the time I had first met Philip.

I wanted his love and tenderness more than I wanted anything. If he felt so strongly about keeping the ayah, then we would keep her. Anything was better than scenes and anger and unhappiness. Even so, I felt a burning indignation at his threat to get the ayah to make up a 'good native brew'.

What would my aunt and uncle have thought, could they have witnessed the scene between us? I had little doubt what they would think about Philip. I lay there, trembling and afraid, with a great loneliness pressing down on me. I reflected that at the beginning of the year I hadn't even known of Philip's existence. And now, because I had met him, I was lying in the heat of an Indian night, thousands of miles away from Wiltshire and Onger House. I thought it impossible that I would sleep that night. I lay awake for hours, straining my ears for the sound of Philip coming upstairs. In spite of everything, though, I finally slept. When I awoke, the house was still and silent.

Philip was not in the bed beside me! Blinking, I suddenly seemed wide awake. There were movements outside the door; the shuff-shuff of the ayah's feet. She would be preparing things in the bathroom. It was eight o'clock by the carved ivory clock in the bedroom. I had instructed the ayah right from the start to get everything ready for me in the bathroom every morning. This was because I had no wish for her to attend to me personally.

There was a tap on the bedroom door.

'The bathroom is ready, memsahib.'

'Thank you,' I said, and heard the shuff-shuff of her feet going away. I slipped out of bed, and stood in the bedroom. How queerly the house was designed upstairs, with one huge room, and two separate dressing rooms and bathrooms. But where was Philip? In his dressing room? I pulled on a wrapper and went to look. He was not there! Something akin to panic began to stir in me. I made a hasty toilette, and hurried downstairs.

The dining room was empty, although the table was laid for breakfast. I hurried into the drawing room and gave a gasp of fear. Philip was slumped across the couch, his face ashen, his body inert. A cry of terror rose in my throat, and I rushed over to him. I gave him a little shake, but there was no response. I felt his pulse; to my great relief it was beating.

'Ayah!' I cried. 'Ayah!' Terror gave a sharp edge to my voice. I could not bear the woman, but in this moment of panic it was to her I turned. She appeared at the door, her dark face impassive.

'The *dorai* is ill,' I said, trying to sound calm. 'Send for Dr Baxter immediately. Quick, do you hear me?'

She stood hesitating at the door.

'Send for the doctor immediately,' I repeated. 'Mr Belvedere is ill.' She disappeared, and I was left with my unconscious husband.

Our quarrel of the previous night was forgotten. Philip was ill — he needed me. And how long had be been lying like this? Was it a stroke or a heart attack? Or worse? The tears rained down my cheeks as I knelt beside the couch. If only he would open those dark eyes — look at me — speak to me!

I held on to his wrist, telling myself that as long as I felt his pulse beating, he would be all right. There was a movement at the door. The ayah stood there.

'I have sent for the doctor,' she said. 'Because you wish it,' she added, with a curious insolence.

'Yes, because I wish it,' I repeated, almost beside myself with fear. 'You were in the house before I was awake. You must have known my husband was here, ill. Why did you not wake me — do something about it before?'

She gave an odd sort of shrug, accompanied by a half smile.

'Send the houseboy in with coffee for me,' I said. 'Don't you bring it.'

If it had not been for the trouble she had caused between Philip and me, I would have dismissed her on the spot. She had known all about him being ill, and yet she had not told me; had not lifted a finger.

Oh, Philip, Philip! Desperately I clung on to his wrist.

After a few minutes Babwah appeared with coffee for me. He put down the tray, and left the room with scarcely a glance at his master. With fear and anguish in my heart, I swallowed a cup of coffee. Oh, Dr Baxter, come quickly, come quickly! For an age I seemed to sit there, holding Philip's wrist. Then I heard voices, a brisk knock at the door, and relief overwhelmed me to see Dr Baxter looking so professional, so unruffled, and so normal, on a morning like this.

'Well, good day, Mrs Belvedere, and what seems to be the trouble?'

To my annoyance, tears began to stream from my eyes again. 'It's my husband — he's ill. I went to bed early — he may have been lying here for hours — the ayah must have known, but she never told me — '

It all sounded very garbled, but how kind the doctor's blue eyes were. He examined Philip in what seemed to me a very cursory fashion. Then he straightened up.

'Now dry your eyes, Mrs Belvedere.

I'll tell you what's wrong with your husband, and I'm sure he won't thank you for sending for me. He's in an absolute stupor with alcohol — that's all. When he comes round he'll have a very bad head indeed.'

'Oh . . . ' I gasped, filled with a mixture of relief and shame. Anger rose in me, too. Anger because I knew the ayah had known what was wrong with him, that was why she had not appeared over-eager to send for the doctor. At the same time, I knew that this must have happened before . . . what a fool I must look in the eyes of the servants. But there was compassion and understanding in David Baxter's eyes.

'Was he drinking last night?' he asked.

'Er — yes . . . well, he usually has a glass of brandy in the evenings,' I said. 'I went to bed rather early last night, and I didn't know until I woke this morning that he hadn't been in bed at all.'

'Well, there's no trace of bottles or

drink in the room, but that is what is wrong with him, I assure you. Try not to take it too seriously.'

I knew then that the ayah had been in the room and removed all traces of drink. Admitted, there was a smell of brandy, but I had not known people could seem ill like this, ashen and inert, through excessive drinking. I felt relieved that Philip was not really ill, and ashamed that David Baxter had witnessed my fear and grief over my drunken husband.

'Perhaps he had a trying day yesterday. It does happen, you know,' he suggested quietly.

'I don't know about that,' I said. 'He'd been to our coffee-garden in Hush Hush Valley, but I don't know anything about it. Philip doesn't discuss business matters much.'

Again the compassion in those blue eyes. For a moment he did not speak, then he said that if I got one of the houseboys to assist him, he would get Philip upstairs to bed.

'It will be less embarrassing for you if he is out of the way,' he added. About a quarter of an hour later he took his leave, after assuring me once more that there was nothing I could do, and that Philip was best left alone.

'If you have no plans for the morning, it might be a good idea for you to go for a drive,' he said. 'Have you been to Devil's Hill, yet?'

'Not yet,' I said.

'Well, my advice to you, Mrs Belvedere, is to order the bullock-coach, and tell the driver to take you there. Have a walk around — it is very pleasant there. Doctor's orders.'

He smiled, and I forced an answering smile. As I stood on the verandah and watched him drive away, there was a desolate feeling in my heart. Indeed, there were many emotions pent up inside me. The beauty of the garden and the cedar trees seemed to mock me. But it was no use standing bareheaded, even in the December sunshine. I ordered the bullock-coach, and put on a sunbonnet. If I came back later in the morning, perhaps Philip would have recovered. Dr Baxter's suggestion for me to go driving was probably a good idea.

As I climbed into the bullock-coach, though, I felt a sense of loneliness which I had not thought possible in a wife. Ramdeen, the driver, stared straight ahead when I told him to drive to Devil's Hill. His swarthy face was impassive as he smoked his foul-smelling beedi pipe. I recalled the conversation at Mrs Radstock's, when they had said the servants knew everything. Suddenly the whole place seemed distasteful to me. I hated Lebanon, the ayah, the other servants — everything.

As the bullock-coach moved off, the thought uppermost in my mind was that things weren't working out the way I had thought they would.

How would Philip be when he woke up? I had no means of knowing. I had been so gay, so confident about our love, and about coming to India. I no longer felt sure about a lot of things, and I had no idea what to do. I could not talk to anyone about the things which were worrying me; I was bound to keep quiet; bound by loyalty to protect my husband.

We were driving up the long, laterite ridge above the river Gawari. It was a big, bare plateau, with yellow *muli* grass on it. Philip had told me that in the rainy season the grass was a vivid green, but I had not yet seen it so. The laterite was black; red when it was first exposed to the earth. To the north it was hard, rough ground which stretched for miles, and seemed little use for anything, but on the south side it sloped steeply into the river. There were coconut gardens, and a belt of paddy and sugar-cane, and there was the Gawari flowing majestically to the sea.

I told the driver to stop. I alighted, and walked slowly along the ridge. It was indeed pleasant, and with a beautiful view of the surrounding countryside. I walked and walked, rejoicing in the faint breeze which blew steadily, and billowed out my muslin dress. I wanted to think; to try and work out how best to deal with Philip. Perhaps, as Dr Baxter had suggested, he'd had a trying day at Hush Hush Valley. If that were so, I had not helped things by suggesting that the ayah should be dismissed. Perhaps I was to blame, perhaps I was doing everything wrong . . .

A kind of panic rose in me at the thought. I quickened my footsteps, almost as if I were running away. Enormous trees loomed up in front of me at the far end of the ridge. There was a walled enclosure there, too.

For a few minutes curiosity made me put my troubles to one side, and I walked forward to examine it. I soon recoiled, though, with a little cry of surprise and disgust. An old man covered with a red blanket was squatting there in the shade of the trees. He wore a yellow turban, and his face was wrinkled and wizened. When he saw me it creased into a hideous grin; he said something in the native dialect. I turned and hurried back to the bullock-coach as fast as I could. Without a word, I climbed back inside, and the driver set off back to the house.

I was determined not to disturb my husband. Let him wake and rise when it suited him. I would have tiffin, and then I would write some letters. The ayah waited at table; shuff-shuff, shuff-shuff. I was not hungry, but I forced the food down, burning my mouth on the strong curry Sam had served.

It was late afternoon before Philip appeared. I looked up enquiringly when he entered the drawing room. He was still pale beneath his tan, and his manner was subdued. However, he looked faintly reassured to see me sitting there, apparently calm and composed. He did not kiss me, and I made no attempt to go towards him.

'I'm sorry about last night,' he said

slowly. 'I really don't know what came over me. I don't remember going to bed.'

'You were carried there this morning,' I told him. 'By Dr Baxter and Babwah.' It was no use trying to keep from him the fact that I had sent for the doctor. He would hear about it, even if I didn't tell him.

'You sent for the doctor?' His voice sounded incredulous.

'Is it so surprising? I found you here apparently in a state of collapse. I didn't know the cause of it. Dr Baxter told me not to worry, but to go for a drive, and let you wake up in your own good time. So I did — I went to Devil's Hill.'

I had decided to appear to have taken it quite calmly. I had kept up the same kind of front for the benefit of the ayah, too. I would let her see that I was made of sterner stuff than she thought. Philip sat down on the couch, and appeared to be thinking things over.

'Perhaps you had a trying day at

Hush Hush Valley,' I added.

'What do you mean?'

'Nothing in particular. Just that you might have had a trying day.'

He gave me a very unsure glance, but said nothing. Then he came across the room, and put his arms around me. He was so contrite, so sorry for his behaviour of the night before, that I felt it was only sensible for me to dismiss the matter. After all, David Baxter had told me not to take it too seriously. And I didn't want to — I wanted us to be friends again.

Locked in his arms, with his voice whispering tender assurances of love, the ugly scene of the night before faded away, along with the shame of his drunkenness. Suddenly we were happy again, happy as people always are when a quarrel has been made up. At dinner that evening, Philip ate little, and drank nothing. We talked about all sorts of things, and discussed plans and invitations for Christmas.

While Philip was in this very contrite

and tender mood, I took the opportunity of mentioning something which I had wanted him to do for some time.

'Do take me round the factory,' I begged. 'I want to see what goes on there. Then if you wanted to talk about it, I would understand more.'

'Oh, very well,' he said at last. 'If your heart is so set on it, I'll take you round the factory. And very dull you will find it, I have no doubt.'

5

My husband kept his word about taking me round the tile works. What I saw there did not reassure me, although I knew nothing about business matters. I walked with him down a succession of long, tiled sheds. A shifty-eyed native, Bango, was in charge. Instinctively I felt that I would not have trusted him a yard.

I asked Philip if he was satisfactory in that position, and he replied that he was as satisfactory as he could hope to get. Bullocks worked a sort of mill to mix the clay, but the presses were hand-worked. There were some kilns and a drying shed. It was a disappointment to me; I had imagined something quite different. At the same time it seemed to me that there was nothing complicated about it. It seemed to me, too, that nobody bothered about anything very much, least of all my husband.

I was sure that the place could be improved enormously. I thought of the money which I had given Philip, money which he had vaguely said was for the factory. Even to my inexperienced eye, it was plain that nothing more than necessary was spent on it. And with that thought came many others. Was Philip always at the factory when he said he was? And the coffee-garden at Hush Hush Valley, what condition was that in? With growing unease I walked round with my husband. Several men were sorting tiles out. There seemed to be a lot wasted to me, and I said so.

'There's bound to be waste,' said Philip tolerantly.

'What about profit?' I pursued.

'Oh dear! What have I married? Fifteen rupees profit on a thousand tiles.'

'And how many tiles do we produce in a day?'

'H'm . . . between two thousand and three thousand. I had no idea you had so much business acumen.'

I had no idea he had so little, but I refrained from saying so. It crossed my mind that my aunt and uncle would not be impressed by the yield from the tile works. Coolies had to carry loaded tiles on their heads down to the boats, another thing which surprised me.

'Why can't we have rails for trolleys to go down with the tiles? It all seems so — ' I broke off.

'Primitive?' suggested Philip, a rather sardonic smile curving his lip.

'Well, yes, I suppose so. It looks as if it hasn't changed for years.'

'It hasn't, I assure you. And it is primitive — much in Sadura is primitive.'

'But the factory could be improved, I'm sure. There are all sorts of modern ideas in factories now — '

'Yes. They cost money, too.'

I didn't want to start another quarrel with him, but I couldn't help remembering that he had told my uncle how well the tile works was doing. I got the impression that it was just keeping going, and that Bango, the foreman, was probably cheating Philip at every opportunity.

A remark of my uncle's suddenly came back to me: 'Your father had a shrewd head on him, and sometimes I think you show signs of having one yourself'. I had known for some time before I met Philip that I wanted something more out of life than most girls in my position were satisfied with. Then he had come into my life, and I had been completely bowled over. But now, after several months of marriage to him, there were things to which I could not close my eyes.

Walking through the tile works with him that day, I had a peculiar moment of revelation. It was very painful; the carefree feeling, the sense that everything was going to be wonderful now we were together, had faded. He drank too much; he was irresponsible about money, and he did not always tell the truth. I was bitterly ashamed of these things. On the other hand, there had been no mother to care for him, and help him while he was growing up.

It must have been a strange household with just his father and the ayah to bring him up. No doubt his father had left everything to the ayah, and I could not imagine her instilling any proper values or standards of behaviour in her charge.

'It's getting dark here already,' I remarked, as we prepared to leave the dimness of the sheds.

'Yes, it's quite dark here by four-thirty — dark all the time in the monsoon.'

I was quiet and thoughtful on the way home. A new maturity seemed to be coming to me, and very quickly. I wanted with all my heart to feel as I had done in those first wonderful weeks after I had met Philip, but I knew I never could again. But if my husband had traits in his character which worried and frightened me, surely it was my task as a wife to try and change him.

If I could make Philip take more interest in the factory — persuade him to let me accompany him there at least once a week. Perhaps we could see about having trolley rails installed from the sheds. If Philip were prepared to put money into the factory, then I would not begrudge giving him it. If he were prepared to drink a bit less . . . if he would show a responsible attitude towards money . . . if . . . if . . .

'I would like to know a lot more about tiles,' I said after dinner that evening. 'I would like to go to the factory every week with you. You are always saying that the servants run the house very well, so if I am absent it will hardly make any difference. I don't just want to sit around listening to the gossip about what goes on in Sadura — '

Philip looked up sharply when I said that.

'Perhaps you are right,' he said, although he sounded rather reluctant. 'Once or twice a week you can accompany me to the works. I've no doubt you will be extremely bored before long.'

I felt encouraged, though, that he had agreed to my proposal. After him making it clear that the ayah was to stay and continue running the house, he must see that I needed an occupation more than just visiting the ladies of Sadura. As I thought about them, I casually asked who the Forrester girl was.

'Why? What have you heard about the Forrester girl?'

'Nothing,' I said. 'Only when the ladies were talking, they mentioned the name of Forrester. Dorothy Forrester, I believe it was. Do you know her?'

He hesitated, looking embarrassed. 'She was a rather hysterical, silly type of girl. Her parents were quite wealthy people, and they were very strict with her, as she was their only child. They would not allow her to mix with whom she chose, and the upshot of it was, she took her own life. After that, her parents left Sadura for good.'

'Did you — like her?' I asked curiously. I don't know what prompted me to say that.

'Like her? Yes, she was well enough in her way.' He dismissed the subject, but I still felt curious, as though I had only heard half a tale. I knew by now, though, that Philip got annoyed if pressed to give more information than he was disposed to.

Sadura was busy preparing for Christmas, and various invitations came our way. It seemed strange to me that there was actually a cricket match on Christmas Eve, in which Philip was taking part. How odd it was to sit in this setting, and watch white-clad figures batting and running in the pleasant sunshine. Stranger still to know that we would be dining out that evening, and that we would be eating turkey and plum pudding.

After the meal, we danced in the spacious drawing room of the judge's house, while the stout Mrs Snow played the piano for us, and a very good pianist she was. It was all very informal, but none the less enjoyable. I was introduced to a Mr and Mrs Dysart, and their pretty daughter, Rosalie, who was about my age. They had been staying in the Nilgiris Hills, but had returned to Sadura for Christmas.

'How are things, Mrs Belvedere?' enquired Dr Baxter in a low voice, when I found myself waltzing with him. 'Are you enjoying yourself on your first Christmas Eve in India?'

'Yes, very much,' I replied. 'I keep thinking about my family and friends back home, of course. It seems funny to have cricket matches on Christmas Eve!'

'And you have had no more trouble?'

I knew what he meant, and felt myself flushing. 'No, none at all,' I said quickly. Over Dr Baxter's shoulder I could see my husband dancing with Rosalie Dysart. She was looking up at him confidingly; what were they talking about? But hard on the heels of that thought came another — as long as he isn't drinking . . .

'It is only natural for you to be thinking about your family in England — one misses loved ones at a time like this,' went on David Baxter. His eyes were sad, and I knew that he must be thinking of his late wife. I found myself wondering what she had been like, and if they had been very much in love.

'Did you go for a drive to Devil's Hill that day as I suggested?' he asked.

'Yes, I did. I thought it was very pleasant up there. I walked along the plateau to the place where there are trees, and a wall. I was curious to know what was there — but there was an old man squatting down with a blanket round him. I hurried back to the bullock-coach.'

Dr Baxter laughed. 'You walked as far as the devil-shrine then. That's what it is, and I've no doubt the old man you saw there was Chitteranjan, the ayah's brother. He's often up there, working his alleged magic.'

'He gave me quite a fright,' I said. I

had never mentioned the incident to Philip, as I didn't wish to mention anything concerning that unfortunate morning.

'He's harmless enough. He lives in one of those little hovels in the bazaar — he squats outside with his lucky charms. And of course, he knows all about the *bhutams* — the devils. Just one of the many queer characters we have living here, white and coloured.'

Dr Baxter always seemed to put things in their right perspective. In his eyes, the ayah's brother was just a harmless old man, not to be taken seriously, just to be tolerated, as other odd things in India were to be tolerated. As we danced together, I reflected that I was glad after all that I had sent for him that morning when Philip had been unconscious. His calm, matter-of-fact manner had assuaged my fears and helped me to adopt a calm manner myself. Later in the evening we played the usual Christmas games; everyone was happy and good humoured. I noticed Rosalie Dysart appeared to be monopolizing Dr Baxter, or was it the other way about? She was pretty and single, and he was a young man, albeit a widower . . .

'I've hardly seen you all evening,' remarked my husband, smiling. 'You are enjoying yourself, aren't you?'

'Oh, yes. Everyone is very nice to me,' I replied. It was true, particularly the older women there, who obviously felt that I would be missing my family on my first Christmas in India. We all sang carols together, and when it was midnight, we kissed all round, as we prepared to depart.

When David Baxter kissed me, it was a quick, gentle kiss; my husband was kissing Rosalie Dysart, and then he turned to me.

'Merry Christmas, Adele.' He too gave me a quick kiss.

'Merry Christmas, darling,' I said, and for the first time that day, I felt the tears prick my eyes.

But it was not because of my family

far away. I don't know what caused my feeling of sadness at that moment. And then I caught David Baxter's eye, and it seemed to me there was an answering sadness in his.

6

The festivities of Christmas and the New Year were over now, and I was not sorry. Twice Philip had been drunk, once in company, and once alone in the house with me. Already I was learning from my husband's face and manner how much he had had to drink. He went from affable to irritable, and from irritable to bad tempered. Beyond that, he sat and drank himself insensible.

I had made the mistake before of trying to argue with him while he was drinking. I hoped now, with the festive season over, he would settle down to a steadier way of life. So I thought to myself early one morning, as I cut flowers in the garden, with the dew still fresh upon them. It was pleasant wandering around at that hour; it was sunlit, but still cool, and everywhere was scented with the perfume of flowers. It was so peaceful, so beautiful, with the splendid cedars spreading their great branches overhead. If only . . . if only . . .

I stood with the flower basket in my hand, thinking that Philip would not rise until late, and when he did, he would be withdrawn and sullen, still reeking of alcohol. After a while he would come round, and be contrite — already I knew the pattern of his behaviour. But if I started going round the factory with him, as he had agreed I should, we could make plans together to improve the tile works. I was determined to do this. I felt sure that I could help my husband in this way, and I really wanted to.

Later that week I tactfully mentioned this to Philip, and he took me to the tile works again. I had a feeling he was making this concession because I had not said anything the last time he had been drunk. I met his chief clerk, Ernest Jones, a Eurasian of about thirty. It seemed to me that he was a conscientious type of man, and was doing his work as well as he could. For a few minutes I was in the poky little office alone with him. I asked him if I could look at the books.

'Certainly, Mrs Belvedere.' He looked rather surprised. Carefully I scanned the books. At school I had always been quick and accurate at figures; I could see the books were very well kept.

'Is all the clay we buy the same quality?' I asked. Ernest Jones gave a non-committal shrug. I knew then that it was not. I had a feeling that there were a number of things he could tell me, but which he was not likely to.

'Whether it is or not, we pay the same price, don't we?' I asked.

'Yes. We pay the same price.' He was saying nothing which he should not, and yet that reply told me a good deal. I knew beyond all doubt that none of the money I had given Philip for the factory had ever found its way there. I resolved there and then that if I gave him any more, I would make sure I knew where every penny had gone. I hated the position I seemed to have been forced into, but some instinct told me that I would have to see to these matters, or the tile works would not survive. Again I walked through the dimly lit sheds, and watched each process carefully.

I had been told by Mrs Snow and some of the other ladies what a lot of pilfering went on in Sadura. I had no doubt that the shifty-eyed foreman, and quite a number of the other workers were guilty in varying degrees. I was pretty sure that the firewood which we had to buy in quantity to fire the kilns was being pilfered. If I mentioned such things to Philip, though, he did not seem to care. It was this which I could not understand.

'I'm going to Hush Hush Valley,' he announced that evening over dinner. The ayah had just left the room after serving us.

'I'll come with you, then,' I said.

Philip put down his fork with an impatient movement. 'For heaven's sake, Adele, why?'

'Don't you want me with you?' I asked, feeling suddenly hurt by his attitude.

'I would prefer to see to the coffee-garden by myself. I should feel a lot freer without having to worry about you. Anyway, you would be very bored.'

'I see,' I said slowly. I thought it best not to make an issue of it. For a while at least, I would let Hush Hush Valley look after itself. I was far from satisfied, though. What went on there?

'How big is the place at Hush Hush Valley?' I asked.

'Oh, it's just a small estate.'

'Is it worth keeping on, then?'

'Certainly. It's doing quite well now.'

I would let him go, then, I thought, and say no more about it for the time being.

'We'll give a dinner party before long,' he said, almost coaxingly. 'We'll invite the Dysarts. They are a nice family.'

I decided that while Philip was

attending to matters at Hush Hush Valley, I would go alone to the tile works, and have a look round by myself. I knew that Bango, the foreman, didn't care for me to go there. Because I was a woman, he thought I should keep out of such things. I suspected, too, that he was afraid I might notice things to which Philip turned a conveniently blind eye. He was probably right about this.

The following day, Philip left for Hush Hush Valley, and after tiffin I put on my sunbonnet, picked up my parasol, and set off for the factory. From the high ridge I could see the river, with the *pattimars*, the rather strange looking native craft with tilting sterns and sloping masts. They could come right up to the jetty for the tiles to be loaded, but the bigger boats, the Gulf *baggalahs*, the Ratnagiri *khotias*, and the *dhows* could not get up the creek. I could see one or two far out to sea. It was a pleasant walk to the factory, situated conveniently close to

Lebanon, and yet not visible from the house.

I walked round to the front entrance, set slightly back from the red, laterite road. I tapped on the door of Ernest Jones' poky little office, and he opened it.

'Oh . . . good day, Mrs Belvedere,' he said in his sing-song voice. He was plainly surprised to see me. 'Can I help you in any way?' He ushered me into the office, and hurriedly dusted a chair for me.

'Good day,' I said, trying to put him at his ease, as he appeared somewhat disconcerted at my unexpected appearance. 'I've just come to have a look round — by myself this time. Mr Belvedere is away on business.'

Ernest Jones' dark, neat-featured face became impassive. 'Yes, quite so,' he said, his voice expressionless.

'Do you know anything about the actual process of making tiles?' I asked him. He looked rather startled.

'Have you any reason for asking that,

112

Mrs Belvedere?'

'None, beyond the fact that I would like certain things explained to me. I thought if you had a few moments to spare — ' I paused, and he looked less apprehensive.

'I know a good deal about the process,' he said. 'My uncle was a tile manufacturer himself some years ago, and I used to assist him. But this factory was so much bigger, and my uncle's output was small, so he gave it up, and now he runs a general store in Sadura. He is glad he gave it up — it was small and ver-ry primitive.' He seemed more at his ease now.

'More primitive than this?' I asked, inclining my head towards the long sheds.

Ernest Jones allowed himself the ghost of a smile. 'Even more so,' he assured me.

His reply gave me what I wanted to know. He knew as much as anyone about tiles, and how they were made. The feeling that I could trust him was strong.

'Will you show me round, then? Have you the time?' I asked.

'Certainly. It will be my pleasure.'

I asked him far more questions than I had asked Philip as we walked about.

'I don't see many workers around the place,' I remarked after a time. 'Where's the foreman?'

He looked somewhat embarrassed. 'Perhaps they have not all commenced their duties yet. I will take you to the sorters. They are all very skilled — they have to be.'

I stood watching them testing the tiles as they came from the kilns. They tapped each one with a short, iron instrument, and from the sound, knew which grade of tile they belonged to, and there were no fewer than five grades. They tested them for flaws, chips and bad colouring at the same time. While we stood and looked, Ernest Jones explained everything very thoroughly.

'Perhaps you would care to walk down to the jetty?' he suggested.

'Yes, I think I would.'

'You know, I expect, that we get the clay in boat-loads to be made into tiles? And a large number of tiles go out from the jetty when they are ready. So it is quite a busy place.'

'It would improve matters if we could have rails, and trolleys to take the tiles down in, instead of men having to carry them on their heads.'

Ernest Jones gave a faint smile, but said nothing. I stood with him, watching the coolies unload a batch of clay.

'Is that good clay?' I asked curiously.

My companion went forward and examined it. 'It appears to be of good quality this time, Mrs Belvedere,' he said gravely. 'As you know, it comes from the river silt.'

I felt a sense of relief, but those two words, 'this time' told me that it was not always of good quality. After some more conversation, we strolled slowly back to the sheds. Firewood for the kiln was piled up in stacks: from behind one of these stacks, Bango suddenly emerged. I caught a whiff of the smell which sometimes tainted my kitchen — and sometimes the ayah's breath. I knew that he had been drinking heavily of cashew-arrack, the potent brew which the natives made themselves.

'You wa-ant something, Mrs Belvedere?' he asked impudently, his voice more sing-song than ever. Repugnance rose in me, and I could sense Ernest Jones' embarrassment.

'It's quite all right,' I said icily. 'Mr Jones has been showing me around.'

'Mi-ister Jones,' repeated Bango. 'He hass perhaps been telling you all about tiles — ' He broke off, laughing unpleasantly.

'I think you had better get on with some work,' I said, and walked on, my face burning.

'Don' look so disgusted,' called Bango. 'You don' need to look so shocked at me — '

'Ignore him, Mrs Belvedere,' said Ernest Jones, hastily. 'I'm sorry you had

116

to meet him like this.'

'So am I,' I said vehemently. 'He's a disgrace. What kind of example is he to the other workers? Does this sort of thing often happen?'

'That I cannot tell you, Mrs Belvedere. You must see, I cannot tell you.'

'I understand,' I said. 'I shouldn't ask you questions like that. That man is impudent; I do not care for him at all.'

He made no reply, but stood looking at me with an odd expression on his gentle face.

'Thank you for showing me around,' I said. 'And for telling me so much. And don't worry — I shan't mention anything I have heard or seen this afternoon.'

I gave him a reassuring wave, and stepped out from the dimness of the tile factory into the bright sunshine. Putting up my shrimp pink parasol, I remembered Bango's parting remark, his voice slurred with drink — 'Don' look so disgusted — you don' need to look so shocked at me'.

The implication was plain. He knew — they probably all knew — about my husband's drinking. I felt suddenly hopelessly forlorn and depressed. Everything seemed cut and dried at Sadura. Everything was cut and dried at the tile works; everything was cut and dried at Lebanon. There was so much I wanted to change, both in the home and outside, but how could I, knowing Philip's attitude? I suddenly noticed a *tonga* drawing up, with Dr Baxter hailing me from it.

'Good day, Mrs Belvedere. Can I take you anywhere?' He looked genuinely pleased to see me, and in spite of everything, I found my spirits lifting slightly.

'I've just been looking round the tile factory,' I said. 'I'm on the point of strolling back.'

'I take it you are not engaged in any particular way, then?'

'Not really. My husband is away on business.'

He seemed to be hesitating. 'I am off

duty for the rest of the afternoon. Would you care to go for a drive?'

I hesitated, too. He laughed. 'I suppose you are thinking it is rather unconventional for a doctor to ask a patient to go driving. Perhaps it is, but never mind. We could drive out on to the ridge if you like.'

To my surprise and dismay, a large lump began to gather in my throat from nowhere. I nodded without replying, and he helped me into the seat beside him. He gave me a swift, sidelong glance, before he clucked the horse into moving.

'You're upset,' he said gently. 'I could see you were when I stopped the *tonga*. When we get away up the ridge, perhaps you can tell me about it.'

I sat there trying to swallow the lump in my throat; longing to confide in this man, and yet dismayed because I wanted to. After all, though, he was my doctor, even if I had no need for him really, from the health point of view. There was something about him which gave me a feeling of security — a feeling which was lacking entirely now I was married. I sat there in silence, fighting back the tears, and he did not press me to speak. We drove along, up the long ridge above the river. When we had a good view out to sea, he reined in the horse.

'I know this is rather unorthodox,' he said. 'But if you are troubled in your mind about things, perhaps it would help you to tell me what is wrong.'

At first I made no reply. When my voice did come, it sounded rather unsteady. 'I don't know if I should be troubled or not,' I said. 'It's not just one thing — it's all sorts of things. I just don't know.'

Dr Baxter cleared his throat. 'I take it you didn't know about your husband's drinking before you married him?'

I knew then that he was well aware of the source of a great deal of my unhappiness. I shook my head, unable to trust myself to speak.

'And is he often like he was when I

called that day? You needn't be afraid to tell me — everything is confidential, you may be sure.'

'Not really often as bad as that,' I said hesitantly. Sometimes he is, and then he's sorry afterwards. He doesn't have any drink for several days, and then he starts having a few glasses of brandy again. Before long he drinks too much, and it starts all over again.'

'And that's the main problem, then?'

His voice was so sympathetic that I couldn't stop myself from pouring out some of my other problems, too. 'I don't like the ayah,' I said. 'Philip won't send her away for my sake, though. He says she's always been at Lebanon, and that's caused friction between us. And he doesn't take the interest in the factory which he should — '

I broke off. I felt I should not be telling David Baxter these things, but they preyed on my mind so much that I felt I must confide in someone.

'You had been visiting the factory by yourself today, hadn't you?'

121

'Yes. Philip's chief clerk showed me round, and explained a lot of things. I would like to see various improvements being made there. I know they would cost money, but I would gladly give it to see it used sensibly.'

'Perhaps this sounds rather impertinent, Mrs Belvedere, but from what you have said, I take it you have private means?'

'Yes. My capital is in England, but I draw the interest on it. I have to travel to Madras for it.'

'I see.' There was a thoughtful note in his voice. He asked me about my life in England, and I found myself telling him all about Onger House, and how I met Philip, and my whirlwind romance with him. Somehow it seemed to relieve my pent-up feelings about everything.

'And now you are here, things are not quite what you thought they would be?'

'No. But I don't know what to do to change anything. I want to take a more active part in things. We have a coffee-garden in Hush Hush Valley, and

I would like to go there. But Philip doesn't seem to want me to. I can't understand his attitude — I can't understand so many things — ' I broke off, feeling that I had said too much again.

For a few minutes we sat there, staring out to sea without speaking. An unexpected feeling of peacefulness seemed to settle upon me.

It was so silent up there. It seemed far away from everyday problems. I knew that Dr Baxter could say very little really to help me, as they were my own personal troubles I was speaking about. Undoubtedly, he had problems of his own. Yet he had driven me up on the plateau, and asked me what was troubling me. It was not just being a good doctor; it was an act of friendship, a hand extended to a stranger in a strange land.

'Try to tackle one thing at a time, Mrs Belvedere,' he said at last. 'You are worrying about everything and nothing.'

'I know that,' I said, and managed a faint smile.

'Things could be worse. Your husband enjoys cricket. I know this bores a lot of ladies, but it's a harmless enough pursuit. Try to encourage him to play whenever possible. He needs the exercise, and, on the whole, among the cricket-playing fraternity at Sadura, there are no bad influences.'

'There are bad influences elsewhere, you mean?'

'Now you are worrying again! Wherever you go, there are bound to be bad influences — '

'The ayah is a bad influence — she's been a bad influence since he was a child,' I broke in passionately.

'You must be a good influence, then,' he said quietly. 'I know it must seem very hard. This is a strange country to you, and the fact that your husband is used to an entirely different way of life is something you will have to accept.'

'There are things I can't accept,' I said.

'We all think that, but we all have to accept a great deal in our lives. And in my experience, you can't have anything without paying for it.'

I sat thinking about his last remark. 'It is very nice of you to drive me up here, and listen to my problems,' I said.

'I'm used to hearing other people's problems, and they are not all health problems, either. Some people just pour them out as soon as I appear. But you are not like that.'

'What am I like?' I asked curiously.

He laughed. 'Like most women, when you make a remark like that. I don't know you very well, but from what I have seen of you — '

'Go on,' I said, suddenly interested.

'I think you are a girl who has led a very sheltered life, and you are finding out it is not quite what you thought. But I don't think you are a weak person. I think you will come through whatever you have to, even though your appearance may belie it.'

'Why — I don't look ill, do I?' I asked.

'No, but you have that pink and white colouring, that rather delicate, water-colour appearance which is deceptive. It probably makes people think you less strong than you are. I don't think you would break in a wind — just bend.'

'It's a comforting thought, anyway,' I said. My companion clucked at the horse, and turned the *tonga* round.

'I'll drive you home now, and I hope I've cheered you up a bit. But if you find yourself worrying, and losing sleep, I shall always be pleased to help you if possible.' His manner, although kindly, was once again that of a doctor. I asked him if he would care to take tea at Lebanon, but he declined, saying he must pay a visit to Sadura hospital.

He gave me a wave as he drove off, and I stood on the verandah, feeling an unexpected pang of loneliness as I watched the *tonga* move out of sight.

7

I sat with Philip at the breakfast table. The ayah had just been in the room; to my surprise I heard the sound of her voice mingled with that of a child's. The door opened, and a little Indian girl of about four ran into the room. She was dressed in a bright orange frock; her black hair was in two plaits, and she stood regarding us with enormous dark eyes.

Philip said something to her in Telugu; she looked nervous, and then the ayah entered the room, took her by the hand, and led her firmly out.

'Well!' I said in amazement. 'Who is that child, and why is she in the house, Philip?'

'It's only Hanna, the ayah's grand-daughter,' he said casually.

'I've never seen her before — I didn't even know the ayah had a grand-daughter,' I said. 'Where does she live?'

'Over in Hush Hush Valley. I brought her back with me for a little holiday. She'll be living in the ayah's house, of course.'

'I never knew the ayah had a family,' I said.

'One daughter. More coffee, please, darling.'

Through the window I saw the child on the verandah. The morning sun caught the bangles on her rounded arms; already she was wearing earrings. But how pretty she was, with beautifully modelled features, and an olive skin. Dislike the ayah though I may, her granddaughter was infinitely appealing.

'She's rather a sweet little thing,' I said.

'Yes. I think so too.'

I was a little surprised that he had taken the trouble to bring this child back with him. If he had known he was going to do so beforehand, why hadn't he told me? Perhaps it had been an impulse on his part, though. I told him that I had visited the factory by myself.

I had delayed telling him, feeling that somehow he would not be pleased.

'The devil you have!' was his comment. 'Really, Adele, you would have been better occupied visiting some of the Sadura ladies. The factory is no place for you to go to alone.'

'I was perfectly all right,' I said calmly. 'Ernest Jones showed me round. He seems very knowledgeable about tiles, and trustworthy, too.'

'Oh, he does?' Philip raised his eyebrows. 'I know where to come then, when any of my employees need a reference.'

'Not *any* of them,' I said tartly. I was nettled by his attitude, and greatly tempted to tell him about Bango, and the condition he had been in when I had visited the factory. Perhaps it was more prudent to remain quiet about it, though, for the time being anyway. Instead, I asked how the coffee-garden was going on. He said that it was well enough. This was the sort of reply which he was prone to make; it could hide anything, and reveal nothing.

Perhaps my best plan was not to bother about the place at Hush Hush Valley at all, and just to concentrate on the factory.

'I could use some of my money to have trolley rails put down, so that they don't have to carry all the tiles down to the jetty on their heads,' I said.

Philip put down his coffee cup. 'What's wrong with carrying tiles on their heads?'

Frustration rose in me. What was the use — what was the use of anything? He had not the slightest intention of improving the tile factory, and whatever the coffee-garden was like at Hush Hush Valley, it would stay like it. It seemed all I could hope for was that he would not get drunk.

'You're playing cricket this evening, aren't you?' I asked, as pleasantly as I could muster, changing the subject.

'Yes. We're playing the Catholic Boys' College, so we'll all have to be on our mettle. Some of our team members aren't as young as we would like, I'm afraid. David Baxter's one of our best players, but he won't be playing today. He'll be at the hospital. He's one of these conscientious types — can't let his patients down.'

'I should think it a bit odd in a doctor if he could,' I said. 'As a matter of fact, I met him when I left the factory, and he drove me out on the ridge. It was quite pleasant.'

'Indeed? You *have* been having adventures in my absence, and no mistake. You never mentioned all this when I came home.'

'You had a headache,' I reminded him.

'Did you ask him in when you got back?'

'Yes, but he had to go to the hospital.'

'As usual. I think he still misses his wife, although he's no need to be lonely. They say in the bazaar that Miss Dysart is interested in him.'

'How on earth do they get hold of this gossip?' I asked.

131

Philip shrugged. 'I've no idea, but they do. Not that one should ever listen to it — I hope that if you should ever hear anything via the servants from the bazaar, you would disregard it entirely.'

'Of course I would . . . but do you think Miss Dysart really is interested in him?'

He laughed. 'Now you are as bad as the bazaar people yourself. She may well be. She is a very pretty girl; most men would not mind her being interested in them.'

Later that day, in the company of several other wives, I sat watching the men play cricket. The boys from the Catholic College were mostly Eurasian, and all were competent players. The 'stations' team as they called themselves, were rather a mixed group of planters and officials, with a sprinkling of Indians who were good players. Among the latter I saw Bango, stone sober today, and apparently in good form.

Rosalie Dysart was there with her

mother. She eagerly scanned the men present. Was it my imagination, or did a look of disappointment cross her face? But if it did, why should I care? I looked at Philip, handsome in his white outfit. He appeared to be happy and engrossed with the game. Yes, I was prepared to encourage him to play cricket, as he enjoyed it so much. If only he would take the factory more seriously . . .

'You look thoughtful,' remarked Mrs Snow. 'You are feeling quite well, I hope? When the really hot weather comes, of course — ' She shook her head, and Mrs Walker waved her fan expressively.

'The heat doesn't bother you young ones so much,' she said. 'It's boredom bothers you. It did me — but a young bride like you should not be bored, Mrs Belvedere.'

'No, I'm not bored,' I said. 'We will be giving a dinner party shortly . . . do you enjoy whist, Miss Dysart?'

'Yes, I like all card games — I've

played whist since I was a child. I like a number of things — I love dancing — ugh! Look at that beastly looking spider — ' She broke off and pointed down. 'That is something I don't like — creepy-crawlies,' she went on.

'I feel exactly the same way about them,' I said. 'My husband laughs at me. I often give a sudden cry when something startles me. And the loveliest looking, most brilliant flowers hide the most horrible, crawling things.'

'That's India,' said Mrs Walker. 'As long as things look all right on the surface, it's better not to disturb them — oh — well played sir!'

She waved her fan appreciatively, and I wondered how many interminable cricket matches she and Mrs Snow had sat through. Miss Dysart's mother began to talk to them both about her health problems, and Rosalie and I strolled round the cricket pitch together. Rather to my surprise, she told me that her mother was over-eager to see her married.

'I've told her I'll marry in my own good time,' she said. 'And I shall be very sure before I do.'

'Mine was a whirlwind courtship,' I said. 'It was love at first sight.' We both stood and watched Philip batting.

'Undoubtedly love at first sight can happen,' said Rosalie. 'But I would never marry a man unless he was doing something really worthwhile. He would have to be someone very special.'

She was extremely sure of herself, and very composed in her manner. She was clearly well aware that she could attract the opposite sex very easily, but she said that she was not prepared to fall in love herself, unless she found what she considered a man sufficiently worthy.

'But you might fall madly in love with someone not at all like you want,' I objected.

'No, I shan't. I shall make up my mind that a certain man is suitable, and I shall get him,' she said firmly.

Suddenly I felt years older than

Rosalie. At one time I had thought things were a great deal simpler than they were. In my case I had fallen in love at first sight, passionately, ecstatically, and I had not cared about anything else. But things weren't simple at all.

'Oh — your husband's out,' said Rosalie. 'A good catch on someone's part, I'm afraid.'

'I'd better go and console him,' I said. 'He won't be very pleased.'

He appeared to have taken it in good part, though. He sat talking to various people clustered outside the pavilion. He stood up as I approached with Rosalie, and was most charming and attentive to both of us.

If only things could always be like this — or did I worry too much? During the next few days, one thing which surprised me was the amount of notice Philip took of the ayah's granddaughter. She was shy with me, which was scarcely surprising, as I could not even speak her language.

Occasionally I could feel her large, grave eyes fixed solemnly on me as I moved about the house and verandah. She was like a tiny, pretty bird, pattering about the place.

We gave the dinner party which Philip had talked about before the last time he had gone to Hush Hush Valley. While I was in the bedroom getting ready, he came in from his dressing room, and dropped a kiss on the nape of my neck.

'You are nice, Mrs Belvedere,' he said, putting his face beside mine, and looking at us both in the mirror. 'I'm going down now, to supervise one or two things while you finish dressing.'

I was nearly ready myself. As usual, I was not able to have my hair in a very elaborate style, not having a maid, but I still preferred things this way, to enlisting the help of the ayah.

Through the door of the dressing room, I could see some of Philip's things dropped on the floor. He was not very tidy. I went into the room. Shirts and other garments seemed to be strewn around the place, and the smell of cigar smoke and eau-de-cologne hung in the hot air. I put some of his things back in the wardrobe, and picked up a crumpled slip of paper from the floor.

It was a bill from a jeweller's shop in London; a bill for a ring costing five hundred pounds. It was charged to my Uncle Henry, and the bill was settled. Bewildered, I turned the receipt over. On the back was written in my uncle's unmistakable handwriting: 'Received with thanks, five hundred pounds from Philip Belvedere'.

It was dated and signed by my uncle. I stood staring at it, trying to make out what it meant. Suddenly it was quite clear. It was a receipt from the jewellers to my uncle, and a receipt from my uncle to Philip. He had charged a five hundred pound ring to my uncle's account, and settled up with him later.

The date on the back was several weeks later than on the jeweller's receipt; it was, in fact, the week after we came back from our trip to London. I remembered the thousand pounds which Philip had asked me to let him have, to help him with his 'unexpected expenses'. He had said it was only until such time as he got back to India, but I had never heard any more about it.

Well, I knew where half of it had gone, anyway. I had bought my own engagement ring. I could just imagine him explaining to Uncle Henry that he wanted to buy me a ring as soon as possible, and asking if he could charge it to my uncle's account, and settle as soon as he was able to get hold of some money of his own.

Uncle Henry would be only too willing; indeed, he probably enjoyed knowing all about the ring before I or my aunt did. I threw the receipt in Philip's wardrobe, and closed the door. I felt dazed, and slightly sick. I knew something now about my husband to which I could no longer shut my eyes. He was completely unscrupulous about money. I took a deep breath of the hot air. It didn't seem to be deep enough, somehow. I went back into the great, lavishly furnished bedroom, and sank down on the couch.

If only my elaborately ruffled dress was not so tight, with such a tiny waist! I must not faint — I simply must not. I sat fanning myself, until, gradually I began to feel better.

I told myself that guests would soon be arriving, and that I would have to entertain them. Later, I could think about Philip's duplicity — later, I could think about a lot of things. I stood up, on legs which seemed slightly trembly. I picked up my fan, and put a fixed smile on my face. The solitaire diamond on my hand winked and sparkled mockingly as I went out of the room and downstairs.

Dr Baxter was among the guests that evening; his eyes met mine with a calm, reassuring look. Miss Dysart was there with her parents; she looked particularly lovely in a diaphanous blue gown.

I noticed her looking admiringly at David Baxter once or twice. Was the bazaar gossip right, then? Certainly he was a man doing a worthwhile task, if that was what she wanted.

I heard Philip laughing just a little too loudly, and straight away the now familiar feeling of fear rose inside me; I felt anger and indignation, too. It seemed to me that he expected to have all his own way. He took my money, and used it without spending it on anything worthwhile. He had very kindly bought me a ring with my own money, yet he would not have one thing altered at Lebanon. I was certain that he gambled; I knew that he drank, and yet he was constantly telling me not to do this, and not to say that.

'Are you all right, Mrs Belvedere?' enquired kindly Mr Snow, who was sitting next to me.

'Yes, I'm very well, thank you,' I said, although it was not really true. In fact, I felt very little like having to be hostess for the rest of the evening. When I rose to lead the ladies into the drawing room, a sudden glance passed between David Baxter and myself.

It told me without a word being spoken that he would do his best to see that Philip did not disgrace himself. I settled the ladies comfortably, and brought out some packs of cards.

'That was an excellent dinner, Mrs Belvedere,' said Mrs Walker. 'Well served by the ayah, too. She keeps going through thick and thin . . . ' She shook her head vaguely, and shuffled a pack of cards.

'Shall we start a game of whist, now?' I asked. 'The gentlemen usually take their time before joining us. We may as well be playing as just chatting about this and that.'

'I think that's a very good idea,' said Mrs Snow. We arranged partners and began to play whist without further ado. She was such a kind, motherly sort of woman; I liked Mr Snow, too. As we played I grew more relaxed, but it was a relief when the rest of the company joined us, and Philip appeared to be all right.

The evening passed off quite well. Philip was an excellent whist player, but by now I knew that he was skilled at all card games. His expert shuffling of a pack of cards alone showed how well used he was to handling them, and not always in a sedate game of whist with friends.

He was a gambler. The realization came on me quite suddenly. He had a friend, Stephen Moray, a planter, whom he would sometimes visit. Stephen Moray was never invited to Lebanon, though, as according to Philip he was a very shy bachelor. I had never met him, probably because he was a thoroughly disreputable character. No doubt they spent their time together drinking and gambling . . .

Snippets of conversation whirled around me as I sat there, but although I heard myself agreeing to go on a picnic, and listening to talk of a ball to be held for Rosalie, it all seemed faintly unreal.

143

I jerked back to the present when I noticed a small figure in the doorway, peeping into the room. It was Hanna, her eyes wide with wonder, her face agog with curiosity.

'Well, what have we here?' enquired Mr Snow jovially. 'Whoever you are, you should be in bed.'

Excusing himself from the game, Philip rose, spoke sharply to Hanna in Telugu, and, taking her by the hand, removed her from sight.

'The ayah's granddaughter,' I explained, as there were several pairs of questioning eyes on me. 'I suppose she's curious, and crept round to the house, knowing we have company.'

'Well, I see no harm in her peeping in,' said Miss Dysart. 'Your husband must think she annoys us.'

Philip appeared at the door, frowning slightly. 'I'm sorry about that interruption,' he said. 'The ayah didn't know she was in the house — she wasn't supposed to be, of course.'

The incident passed off without

further comment. Somehow I did not believe that the ayah had not known Hanna was in the house. And why had I never heard before about the ayah having a daughter? She must have lived with her mother before she got married, which meant Philip must have known her from being a child. Yet he had never mentioned her until he had brought Hanna back for a stay.

'It's been a most pleasant evening,' said David Baxter, as the guests made their farewells. I had a sudden wish that I could talk to him; tell him all my fears and worries. We had not had a chance throughout the evening to exchange any conversation apart from what was shared by the rest of the company.

Philip and I waved from the verandah. It was a windless, starlit night. I saw my ring sparkle momentarily, and it brought back the depressing realities which I had to live with.

'Were there any comments when I removed Hanna from the room?' asked

Philip, as we went into the house together.

'No,' I said rather shortly. 'Why should there be? Why should people be interested in a little native girl? Nobody was the least inconvenienced by the child's appearance in the drawing room.'

Philip appeared relieved. He sat down and lit a cheroot. He also poured himself out a stiff brandy. I sat watching him with mixed feelings. I wanted to cry out — why had he bought me a ring which he could not pay for? Soon we would be taking the train to Madras again, and I would call in my bank there, for some money. And I knew that he would ask me for some, and make up some story about the tile works needing it, or perhaps even the coffee-garden at Hush Hush Valley. I remembered how I had said that marriage was for sharing. But what were we sharing?

Little enough, from what I could see. I was not *close* to him, somehow. I knew that I could not bring myself to tell him that I had found that ring receipt. If it had just been an isolated incident I could have overlooked it. But the business of the engagement ring was typical of his attitude.

'Why are you looking at me like that?' he asked, pouring out more brandy.

'I'm just wondering if you're going to sit and drink yourself into a stupor,' I said, anger tingling through me.

'It's quite likely that I shall,' he replied coolly.

'I suppose I should be grateful that our guests have gone.' There were so many emotions churning round inside me that I could feel myself on the edge of a bitter quarrel. My angry grief and bewilderment that he should have turned out the way he had seemed as though it must overflow somehow.

'*I'm* grateful that they've gone — these dinner parties and things are mostly for your sake. Oh, I quite enjoy a game of cricket, I admit. But personally

I would as soon spend a few hours in the company of Stephen Moray as I would with the more élite society to be found in Sadura.'

'I'm sure you would,' I replied. 'You probably have similar ideas on enjoying yourselves.'

'What do you mean by that?' Philip's face took on a vicious expression. Evidently I had struck home with a chance remark.

'Gambling — drinking,' I said, as coolly as I could muster, although I could feel myself beginning to tremble.

'What a little prig you are! So self-righteous, standing in judgement — '

'Never mind about that,' I said, still trying to keep calm. 'You gamble and drink at every opportunity — ' I broke off, as other accusations were trembling on my tongue.

'Yes, I gamble and drink at every opportunity,' he agreed, draining his glass of brandy. 'As you're my wife you might as well get used to the idea — '

'And I suppose I might as well get

used to the idea that you haven't a grain of interest in the tile factory?'

'I can think of other ways of spending my time. Pleasanter ways.'

'I've no doubt you can,' I said. 'And other ways to spend our money, than on improving the factory — ' I broke off, hearing a slight movement outside the door. I rushed across the room and opened it, my face burning with anger. The ayah stood there. 'What do you want?' I asked, my dislike and mistrust of the woman brimming over.

'Er — nothing, memsahib. I have finished in the house. I go now.'

'Yes, do. And kindly don't listen outside doors in future,' I added, closing the door on her.

'There's no need to vent your spleen on the ayah,' remarked my husband. 'She was doing no harm.'

'Of course not — merely listening at the door. Small wonder these native servants are reputed to know everything — they are highly skilled at the art of spying.'

'For a wife of a few months, you find many faults in your household.'

'Yes, I do, don't I? Perhaps I don't like all the spying and lying that goes on.' I walked out of the room, because I could see we were exchanging bitter words without getting anywhere.

Also, I could feel tears of frustration and anger welling up, and I was determined not to give way. I walked up the stairs and into our bedroom, with a sense of depression and defeat. In the light of the oil lamp, I sat at the lovely dressing-table, and prepared for bed.

I took off my engagement ring — the ring which I had bought myself, and saw the stone leap with fire as I did so. I had no doubt Philip would sit downstairs, probably all night, drinking. What was I to do? Oh, God, all my life was going wrong, and how was I going to cope? I bowed my head, and gave way to a few minutes bitter weeping. There would be another sleepless night for me . . .

To my surprise, though, I had no sooner undressed and got into bed, than I heard Philip's footsteps on the stairs. He entered the room, and went into his dressing room, where he stayed for quite a long time. Eventually he slipped into bed beside me.

In spite of my unhappiness and growing disillusionment, I longed with all my heart to feel his arm go round me. If only I could understand why he behaved like this — if only he would admit that he had these weaknesses, and would make a genuine effort to conquer them.

I lay there for a long time, thinking bitter and hopeless thoughts. After a while I could tell by Philip's breathing that he was asleep. He did not lie awake thinking and worrying about me as I lay awake thinking and worrying about him.

8

About a fortnight later, Philip again went to Hush Hush Valley, taking Hanna back with him. He had been rather quiet since our last dinner party, when I had spoken so bitterly about his habits.

We had not discussed the quarrel any further, or made it up properly, but hopes began to rise in me that what I had said had not fallen on stony ground. Twice he had asked me if I wanted to accompany him to the factory, and I had been pleased about that.

On both occasions I called into the office, and had a brief talk with Ernest Jones. In spite of my husband's lack of interest, I had still not given up the idea of spending money on improving the factory. I always looked forward to my visits to Madras; I wondered if Philip would ask me for money again the next time I went to my bank there. I had no doubt he would, and that it would be either frittered away on drink or gambling, or else used to pay his debts. Should I make a firm stand, and refuse to let him have any money, unless I supervised what became of it? Even as I thought this, I had a feeling of resentment that I had been forced into this position. I felt that it was his place to look after our interests, our money, and our factory.

Willy-nilly, the thought came to me, what would my aunt and uncle think about things, if they knew the true state of affairs? And hard on that thought came another — they must never know.

Another thing was worrying me, though. I seemed to be suffering from a growing feeling of lassitude. It was an effort to get up in the mornings, and I was always ready to rest after tiffin. I thought it was probably the climate taking its toll. My face seemed to have a drawn look, which it never used to.

Perhaps I was worrying too much about things altogether.

I lay on the couch in the drawing room after tiffin. I was expecting Philip back from Hush Hush Valley that evening. I must have fallen asleep, because I woke with a jump, feeling bewildered at first as to where I was. Then I realized I was in the drawing room, not the bedroom. For a few moments everything seemed a little unreal. What was I doing in this strange house in India?

I didn't belong there — I never would. I wanted to be back home with Aunt Margaret and Uncle Henry. Everything pressed down on me like a dead weight; Philip's changed attitude, his improvident ways, and his deceptions. This house . . . where the ayah held sway, and I was not the mistress except in name . . . this house, where I was the foreigner . . .

There was a shuff-shuff outside, a tap at the door, and the ayah stood there with a tea tray. I was damp with perspiration, and felt suddenly nause-ated. The room seemed to be spinning around. Surely I was not going to faint? No, I would not faint, nor be sick in front of the ayah. Her eyes seemed to be mocking me as she put the tray down, and left the room. The face of Philip's mother seemed to mock me too, looking down from its gilt frame. I wondered what problems she had faced in this house, and if she had been happy.

Well, I was not happy, and moreover, I was not well, either. I felt drained of strength.

When Philip arrived home, he was in a sullen, withdrawn mood. I wanted to tell him that I had missed him, and that I had felt unwell in the afternoon. It was plain that he was not interested, though; he answered my first greetings with indifference. Frustrated, I remained silent throughout the meal, not even bothering to ask how things were at Hush Hush Valley.

My husband didn't volunteer any

information, either. He sat silent, too, while the ayah waited on us. It was going to be one of his drinking nights; I knew all the signs by now.

'I think I would like a drive out to Devil's Hill,' I said. 'I felt so tired this afternoon, I slept.'

'Really?' was my husband's response.

'Would you care for a drive out there?' I went on.

'I would not. I've done enough travelling today.'

'Very well,' I said coolly. 'I'll get Ramdeen to take me in the bullock-coach.' If Philip had stopped drinking, if he had made the least sign that he had wanted me with him, I would not have gone. Despite my outward appearance of calmness, my feelings were in a turmoil.

My husband was going to sit and drink himself into a stupor, I knew that. It would make no difference if I were in the house or not. Why, then, should I have to sit and watch him, when I could just as well be out? Still keeping my composure, I ordered the bullock-coach. In the bedroom, seeing my wan reflection in the mirror, I pinched some colour into my cheeks. A few minutes later I sat in the coach as it proceeded at a leisurely pace towards Devil's Hill.

It was a popular spot for evening drives. At a certain point, people got out and walked, and exchanged greetings with each other. I thought of the first time I had driven there, on Dr Baxter's advice. I thought too, of the afternoon when he had met me as I left the factory, and had taken me there in his *tonga*. I had been there since with Philip, and once a whole party of us had met there for a picnic. As we got on top of the ridge, I noticed quite a number of other people strolling up and down while their bullock-coaches waited.

It might look a little odd if I walked about unescorted on the ridge in the evening. But the bitter thought arose, my husband hadn't wanted to come out with me; I was alone, so why should I consider what people thought? The next moment I was out of the bullock-coach and walking along, taking deep breaths of the pleasantly cool air. High up like this, there was a feeling of freedom and lightness. Back at Lebanon there seemed only to be unhappiness. The beauty of the scenery, and of the evening, before the tropical, starlit darkness fell, had a calming effect on me.

I was startled when, quite suddenly, a party of four turned round from close to the devil-shrine, and I recognized Mr and Mrs Dysart, their daughter Rosalie, and Dr Baxter. I felt myself flushing under their combined gazes; it was quite clear that they thought it a little odd for me to be there by myself.

They all greeted me very pleasantly. 'Well, what have you done with your husband?' enquired Mr Dysart jovially.

I forced a cheerful smile. 'He's been away on business all day,' I said hastily. 'I felt like a drive out, but he's rather tired.'

How pretty Rosalie Dysart looked in her filmy blue gown. I guessed Dr Baxter had dined with the family that evening, and they had all driven out for a stroll on the ridge afterwards. I had no doubt that Miss Dysart was interested in David Baxter, but it did not necessarily mean that he returned the interest. As we stood talking, though, I had a strong feeling that if she made a match of it with him, her parents would be well pleased.

A pang of envy shot through me. I felt so alone, having to make conversation with a smile on my face, while all the time I knew that my husband was sitting in the house, drinking, sullen and morose. And yet, only a few months ago, I would not have envied any girl . . .

'Are you feeling quite well, Mrs Belvedere?' came Dr Baxter's voice, and there was a genuine note of concern in it.

'Yes — well, no — that is, I've felt a bit listless lately,' I said, feeling rather embarrassed. 'I suppose it's the heat.'

'Um. You look a bit peaky to me,' was his comment. 'I'll call round one day next week, and you can tell me all about it.'

I was on the point of thanking him, but declining his offer, when I decided it might be a good thing. It was true that I didn't feel very well, and that was not helping me to cope with matters at home.

'I suppose Philip will be at the cricket match this week?' enquired Mr Dysart.

'Yes, I should think so,' I said. Just at that point, I saw Judith Radstock and her husband approaching us. The greetings and the unexpected company did me good, but how happy I would have been if only Philip had been with me . . .

Nevertheless, it was good to get out of the house, away from the rule of the ayah, and the many problems which beset me. Sitting in the bullock-coach some time later, on the way back to Lebanon, the depression returned, though.

I knew that Philip would be sitting drinking when I entered the house. What had happened in Hush Hush Valley to make him come home in such an unpleasant mood? Probably nothing — it was just the way he felt. I thought about Hush Hush Valley, and wondered what it was like there, and why it was called that. Philip had said that it had an Indian name, but nobody used it. I knew the direction it lay in, but the road there always looked mysterious and frightening, dark, beneath the towering Ghats. Why was Philip always so insistent that I should not accompany him there? Still, if I did, there would probably be no good result from it, most likely the coffee-garden was as neglected as the tile factory. And if I started to pester him to improve things, it would only lead to more friction.

I reflected that I seemed to be completely trapped. How had it all come about, and what had I done wrong? Bracing myself for whatever might happen, I entered the house.

Everything was as I had anticipated; Philip was sitting drinking. He raised his head when he saw me.

'Have you had a good drive?' he asked, his voice sarcastic.

'Very pleasant,' I replied, coolly. 'I met quite a number of people who had driven out, and were walking on the ridge. I met Mr and Mrs Dysart, and Rosalie — and Dr Baxter, and Mr and Mrs Radstock — '

'How nice for you,' he broke in. 'You would be able to tell them that I was back in the house, drinking.'

'Yes, it was nice for me. But I didn't tell them that you were back in the house, drinking. There are some things which I prefer not to talk about. I was grateful for some pleasant company.'

I could scarcely believe that it was me standing there, saying these cutting things to my husband of a few months. If he had put down his glass, and tried to pull himself together, instead of sneering at me, I would not have done so. If only he had shown me some of

162

the tenderness I longed for, I would have overlooked many of the things which had shocked and wounded me.

In his present mood it was no use continuing the conversation at all. I didn't know if he intended to play cricket that week or not, and I felt I didn't care. It was all so hopeless. Without saying anything further, I picked up a book, with the intention of reading it in my bedroom. I sat down, feeling suddenly nauseated. The room was spinning around again.

'I don't feel very well,' I managed to say.

'You had better go to bed, then,' said my husband. 'It doesn't suit you to go driving alone in the evening.'

I wanted to make a suitable retort, but suddenly I felt too ill to care. Everything turned black, and I lay back on the couch. I came round with the ayah holding a burning chicken feather under my nose. I was sobbing uncontrollably, and shivering.

'She's all right now,' said the ayah.

'Wait a lit-tle while, and we'll get her to bed, Mr Phi-lip.'

I felt too ill to speak at all. Between them, they helped me upstairs and into the bedroom.

'Prepare something to make her sleep,' said my husband. 'I'll help her into bed.'

He did so without speaking. The ayah had left the room; as Philip leaned over me I could smell the alcohol on his breath. I turned my head away, nausea rising in me again. I lay in bed, my eyes half closed, with Philip a shadowy figure in the room. He sat on the couch, and later, the ayah returned with something in a glass.

'Drink this up,' said Philip. 'It will make you sleep — you'll feel much better when you wake up.'

'No — I don't want it,' I muttered, half turning away.

'Do drink it, Adele.' His voice seemed softer now, without the note of sarcasm in it. He slipped his arms round me, and held the glass to my lips.

The liquid had a strange, sweet, indescribable taste. I drank it, and lay back on the pillow. I could hear the ayah and Philip talking in low voices; even though a great drowsiness was overcoming me, I knew that they were not speaking English. My arms and legs felt as heavy as lead. Suddenly I didn't care about anything . . .

Then I was dreaming; hideous nightmares tormented me, causing me to cry out in terror. Snakes seemed to be swarming through the bedroom, crawling over the bed and wrapping themselves around me. It was a dreadful torment, an endless night of horror; I felt a hand clasping mine, and saw a kind pair of eyes looking at me. They were not Philip's eyes.

'Dr Baxter!' I cried, and poured out all my miseries and problems; all my worries about Philip, my disillusionments, and my fears for the future. Someone was gently shaking me.

'Mrs Belvedere! Mrs Belvedere!'

I suddenly realized that I was awake

in the bed, and Dr Baxter was in the room with me. I tried to collect my thoughts.

'You've been having nasty dreams,' he said sympathetically. 'I'm here, and you're perfectly safe — no snakes, no nothing.'

I gave a long, gasping sigh. I could feel the perspiration running from me in little rivulets.

'I thought it was a dream — you being here,' I murmured.

'No, it's no dream.' He sat on the couch. 'Your husband sent for me first thing this morning. He said you had been ill last night, and that you were sleeping restlessly. I came and took your temperature while you were still asleep, and said I would call back later. It's nearly tiffin time now, and you're just waking up. I thought you looked a bit peaky when I saw you on the ridge. When you come round a bit, I'll see if there is anything causing you to feel ill.'

'I haven't felt well for the last month or so,' I said. 'I suppose it's the climate.'

'The climate can't be blamed for everything,' said Dr Baxter, his blue eyes looking at me searchingly. 'Have you been feeling very tired lately?'

'Yes. Yes, a sort of lassitude — I can't explain it . . . '

'Can't you?' There was a faint, rather sad smile on his face, and then he became professional again. Ten minutes later he told me what was ailing me.

'Just rest as much as possible. You must expect a certain amount of discomfort in the early stages. But I can assure you there is nothing to worry about, Mrs Belvedere. You must take care of yourself, and I will take care of you when the child is born.'

I lay back on the pillows without speaking.

'These things happen, you know,' he said quietly. 'I'm sure your husband will be pleased — and all the ladies in Sadura will make a fuss of you.'

I managed to smile when he said that.

'I'll send your husband up to you.'

He left the room.

After a while the door opened again, and Philip stood there. He walked into the room, looking somewhat embarrassed.

'Dr Baxter says you are all right now,' he said, with rather an ashamed glance at me.

'Yes, I'm all right,' I said slowly. 'I'm having a baby, though. Did he tell you?'

'No. But he said you had some interesting news for me. I guessed it would be that.'

He sat down on the bed, and took my hand in his. From the bits I had heard about such things, and the books I had read, I should have felt great joy at that moment. My husband should have been thrilled at being told the wonderful news. But he merely sat holding my hand with a rather hang-dog expression on his face.

I didn't feel any great joy, either. I probably would have done if Philip's behaviour had not caused me such concern. Would a child change him, though?

I remembered how he had played with the ayah's grandchild. A man who was indifferent to children would not have done that.

Hope rose in me again, as strong as ever. I squeezed his hand, and he bent and kissed me. And I felt at that moment that things would surely be better; that Philip would settle down, and that the child would bring joy when it came.

9

The next few weeks were not easy ones for me. Despite the fact that Dr Baxter had assured me that I was a perfectly healthy mother-to-be, I still felt very tired and drained, with unpleasant attacks of nausea.

My visits to the factory ended. Somehow I no longer felt much interest; the forthcoming child was such a tremendous event to look forward to that other things got thrust to one side. Philip seemed very quiet these days. He said that he was looking forward to the child being born, and I hoped that this was so.

Dr Baxter had told me to keep as calm and unworried as possible, for the sake of the baby, as well as my own.

'I give this advice to all my patients expecting a happy event,' he said. I wondered uneasily if this were so. I remembered in my dream, seeing his face, and telling him all my problems and worries. Had I still been dreaming? Or had I in fact, blurted out everything to him? I had no way of knowing; certainly I could not ask him. If I did, he would merely assure me I had been dreaming, whether or no.

Philip and I planned to go to Madras, where I would again visit my bank.

'You had better keep the allowance for yourself, this time,' he said. 'You will need things for you and the baby.'

His attitude seemed to be that he was doing me a favour by allowing me to keep my own money, instead of giving it to him to squander. If only he had been different; if only he had studied my wishes, and had tried to improve the tile works. When we had got married, and I had talked of sharing, it had never crossed my mind that I had married a man who was, I suppose, what Uncle Henry would have called a 'waster'.

In my limited experience of the

world, the people close to you paid their bills; anything else was unthinkable. Besides, I could not believe that the man I had fallen in love with on sight could be anything else but truthful and honourable. Naturally, I had heard stories about girls being 'taken in' by men. But I had always thought that those sort of things could only happen to other people, not to me.

I had decided not to tell Aunt Margaret about the child just yet. I knew that I would get letters with pages of advice as soon as I did. She was so loving, so full of concern for me. I had been hard put to conceal my impatience at the many lectures I had received from her and my uncle, before I had married Philip.

It was a galling fact, but how right their warnings and strictures had been. I still continued to write cheerful letters to England, though, to say that I was settling down, and all was well. It was too early for my condition to be made known to other people yet. I was quite certain the ayah knew, though.

Sitting watching a cricket match one day, Mrs Snow, who happened to be sitting next to me, asked me in a low voice if it was true that I was expecting a child.

'Well . . . as a matter of fact, yes. But how did you know?'

'I've thought you looked a bit out of sorts lately — and I did hear something. These things leak out, my dear. In any case, one cannot keep it a secret for very long. I am happy for you, and I hope it will have a settling effect — ' She broke off, as if she had said enough, and I did not ask her what she meant.

Instead, I had a curious feeling of closeness to Mrs Snow, just for a few minutes. Somehow, I felt that she knew all was not what it appeared on the surface, as far as my life in Sadura was concerned. She had known Philip from his childhood; how much more she must know about him than I did!

'I won't mention it to anyone, if you

prefer to keep it quiet a bit longer,' she said. 'When will it be born?'

'In the autumn,' I said.

'I am sorry you will have to go through the heat of July, and the monsoon, then. But you are young, and you will survive. And the ayah will take care of it — '

'No!' I cried. 'Not the ayah!'

'But, my dear, who else?'

'I would prefer to take care of my baby myself,' I said, a trifle lamely. It was something which I had not discussed with Philip, because I had a feeling that it would lead to another quarrel about the ayah. I had decided that I would devote all my time to the baby, while it was very young, at all events. The ayah could run the house, and have nothing to do with the child.

'You won't find that an easy task, besides, everyone has an ayah for the children . . . I think I understand how you feel, though. I know of a very nice young girl — a Christian, too, who would look after your baby well, during the day, and if you wanted to go out in the evenings. You could have your own little ayah, perhaps?'

'Thank you, Mrs Snow,' I said. 'I would not mind that.'

'A girl has the right to choose her own nursemaid for her children, wherever she is living,' she went on. 'And there are times, my dear, when one must stand up for one's rights.'

By a kind of unspoken consent, we changed the subject. But Mrs Snow's words remained in my mind. It seemed to me I had little enough say in the way my household was run, but things were going to be different concerning my unborn child.

I knew that I could be independent of a lady's maid now; although the ayah prepared my bath, and did other things of a like nature, she never performed any of the more intimate offices which comprise the duties of a proper maid. If I could manage to take care of my clothes, and do my toilette unaided, then I could take care of my baby, too, when it came.

Nevertheless, the prospect was a bit worrying. I thought of girls I had known who had married and had a baby, and the enormous commotion the arrival of these scraps of humanity appeared to cause. There was always a monthly nurse in attendance, and a nannie ready to take over, and a nursemaid, too, to do the rougher work. A baby took an awful lot of looking after, and if I spent too much time with the child, Philip might not be pleased.

If I had a good ayah of my own, though — and Mrs Snow appeared to know of one — I could safely leave the child in her care for part of the time. I consoled myself with the thought that I had plenty of time to think about these things, before I made any definite arrangements. And once the child was born, Philip might be different altogether. He might become a proud father, and face up to his responsibilities like a man . . .

The hope of a happy future rose in

me again. Philip and I went to Madras together. Despite the heat, I enjoyed the change. There was a thrill in buying for the expected child, too. I bought a quantity of filmy white material to make tiny gowns and dresses with. I was determined to sew them myself. When the baby was older, I would have the *darzi* from the bazaar to help with the clothes making. He was the proud owner of the first sewing machine ever seen in Sadura, and he was greatly in demand. He went from house to house, staying with one family for a week or a fortnight at a time, during which his busy machine would whirr away on the verandah from dawn till dusk.

I knew that I ought to tell Aunt Margaret about the baby, yet still I hesitated. The later she knew, the less time she would have to worry and fuss. Philip seemed to be behaving extremely well since he had known about the child. There had been no evenings when he had sat silently drinking, although occasionally he had gone out to visit his planter friend, and had come home late. There had been no arguments between us, though. When he left the house, saying that he was going to the factory, I never commented. In my heart I did not believe that he always went there, but I could see no point in raising the matter with him.

I told myself that once the child was born, and I was well and strong again, I would be able to tackle a number of things which I was not bothering about at present.

'I'm going to write and tell my aunt and uncle about the baby,' I informed Philip at tiffin, one day.

'Yes, they'll have to know sometime,' he said, a trifle absently.

'Later on, we will have to turn my dressing room into a nursery.'

'Yes, I suppose so. That should be easy enough to do.'

'I shall need a cot, and things like that — ' I paused. For a moment I wondered whether to take the bull by the horns, and say I would be engaging the services of an ayah. But I did not know how Philip would take it, and I felt I could not face the prospect of an argument about it just then.

The ayah came in silently with the dessert. I never felt private while she was in the house. I always had the feeling that she was lurking behind doors, listening.

'We're expecting a big load of clay — I'm going to the factory shortly,' said Philip. 'Fattorini's men are trying to outbid me on most fronts, now.'

'Fattorini's?' I asked, sudden fear going through me.

'Yes. You know the Italians have a factory the other side of the town? Not so conveniently situated as ours, for loading and unloading, though. But I've heard they intend to expand it — ' He broke off, as if he had said more than he intended.

Then he continued — 'I hadn't bargained for the price of clay rising, Adele. We will have to charge more for tiles. It's going to make things a bit difficult all round.' He sat looking down at his plate.

'Well,' I said, after a pause during which time a lot of thoughts were going round my head. 'What can we do about it? Do you need more money — ?'

He looked up, and reaching across the table, gave my hand a quick squeeze. 'It's come at such an awkward time. I know you need money for yourself and the baby — '

'If you have to pay out more to compete with the Italians, it's important that you should be able to,' I said. In my heart, I was thankful that he was at least showing some signs of caring about the tile works.

'I'm glad you realize that, Adele. Just lately things don't seem to have gone satisfactorily at all.'

'Don't worry about it,' I said. 'Of course we want the tile works to flourish — we have the baby's future to think of now.'

'It's a pity — ' Philip broke off without finishing.

'What is a pity, dear?'

'I was going to say it's a pity your capital is all tied up in England, at a time like this.'

I sat without speaking, my feelings very mixed. Were we going to have to battle to save the tile works? A fiercely protective feeling towards my unborn child rose in me. It seemed as if Philip *was* changing, as if the prospect of fatherhood was making him see things in a different light.

'There's not much I can do about that,' I said at last.

'It's tied up in various investments, I know. But Uncle Henry made it plain that it stays in England.'

'It's ridiculous when you're living in India,' went on Philip moodily.

'Well . . . ' I said. There was a long pause, and then I spoke the thought which had been in my mind for some time now.

'We don't *have* to live in India,' I said. In a sudden flash I saw the hills of home; Wiltshire in the springtime, green grass and fresh breezes; England . . .

'I do,' said Philip, and with those two words he effectively stopped my winging fancies. Yes, he wanted to live in India, but his wife's money was tied up in England, I thought bitterly. But perhaps I was judging him too harshly; he seemed genuinely concerned about the tile works.

'And the estate at Hush Hush Valley? Is that doing reasonably well?' I asked.

'Reasonably well.' He did not seem disposed to talk about it. 'Anyway, dearest, I will try and outstrip the Italians. One can only do one's best. Now what are you going to do while I'm out?'

'Sit in the long-chair and sew,' I said with a smile. 'It's quite a restful occupation.'

He kissed me before leaving the house. I sat in the drawing room, in the stifling heat. Overhead, the punkah, a light, plaited mat, swung to and fro, as Babwah sat on the verandah, pulling the cord which controlled it. Sometimes he would get tired, and stop for a while, and the air would press down like a sticky blanket. I sat with damp hands, putting pin tucks and inserting lace in a tiny white gown. It seemed impossible that a human being could be so small, but at the same time it seemed impossible that I could give birth to anything so big.

I sat there, thinking about one thing and another, while I sewed. It was a complete surprise when the ayah announced Dr Baxter, and he walked into the drawing room.

'Good day, Mrs Belvedere — I hope I find you fairly well?'

'Oh, yes, thank you.'

He put down his wide-brimmed hat, and sat in the chair opposite mine. He had told me that he would call occasionally to see how I was. As usual, his presence was reassuring.

'I see you are already making preparations,' he went on, smiling, his eyes on the little gown I was busy with.

'Yes.'

'Just as well to have everything ready

as soon as possible. Later, with the heat to contend with, it will be too much to bother yourself with.'

'Excuse me — one moment,' I said. I rose, walked to the door and opened it, to reveal the ayah standing there. 'I would like some tea for Dr Baxter and myself,' I said coldly. 'And tell Babwah to keep the punkah going.'

Even that slight exertion brought beads of moisture to my forehead. As I turned round, I saw the doctor dabbing his face with his handkerchief. He laughed, and it occurred to me that in spite of the fact that he often looked serious, he had a very infectious laugh.

'It will be hotter than this before it's finished with us,' he said cheerfully. 'It was kind of you to order some tea — it has a cooling effect after you've drunk it. You're losing that drawn look, I'm pleased to see. I suppose the ayah was listening outside the door?'

'As a matter of fact, she was,' I said.

'I've caught her doing that again and again.'

'And I suppose she still does it . . . I take it that she knows about the addition to the family?'

'I've no doubt she does,' I said, 'but not from me.' There was a short, slightly uncomfortable silence. 'I don't want her to have anything to do with my baby when it comes,' I went on. 'I don't feel as though I could trust her with my child.'

'Why is that?' he asked quietly.

'I can't really say. There's something — oh, I don't know — something sinister about her. And that awful old man, the devil-dancer, is her brother — '

Somehow I felt I had to tell him these things, although they hardly came under the heading of health problems. I seemed to be in rather an awkward position with Dr Baxter. I knew that he was sympathetic towards me, but it was difficult to know how much I could tell him, without just seeming an imaginative woman, prone to fears and fancies.

'There is time to decide these things,' he said. 'As for her brother, he is having a wonderful time at the moment, frightening people to death.'

'Frightening them? About what?'

'He has forecast great trouble to come with the monsoon this year. Great floods will come, so he says, and disease to follow, for those who survive the floods. He really is a cheerful character — I don't know what the bazaar would be like without him.'

'Have there been floods before when the monsoon comes?' I asked.

'I believe they had very bad floods here once — about twenty years ago.'

I sat thinking about this.

'Of course, the rivers get very dried up before the rainy season, and then they get full to brimming over, so there is always a bit of flooding. Anyway, according to Chitteranjan, we shall all be washed away. You should be all right, though, being on a hill well above the mouth of the river.'

'Yes, but the tile works . . . ' I mused.

Dr Baxter laughed. 'My dear Mrs Belvedere, put the idea out of your head. That old man enjoys a feeling of power here; it is bad enough that the poor ignorant natives believe him, and believe in his magic working. If you pay him, he will work magic for you, and he will always work magic for a bottle of brandy.'

At this point the ayah appeared with a tea tray. I was glad the doctor had called. It was ostensibly a professional visit, but we talked about a number of things as we drank the Darjeeling tea. Somehow Miss Dysart's name cropped up; there was talk of a ball for her twentieth birthday.

'She is very pretty,' I said.

'She is indeed,' he agreed.

For a moment I sat without speaking. A strange pang stirred in me, not of jealousy, but of envy. Envy of the pretty Miss Dysart. Everything lay ahead of her, and she was so confident, so sure of herself. I had no doubt that Dr Baxter admired her; what man would not? I put down my cup with a little sigh.

Dr Baxter stood up.

'I am pleased to see that you are keeping well, anyway. Don't cut down on your social life more than necessary. If it's too hot in the day to take any exercise, drive up on to the ridge in the evening, and take a walk. There is always a breeze there. I shall see you again in the near future. Meanwhile, keep on taking care of yourself. I must go now.'

I walked slowly back to the drawing room, after seeing him off on the verandah. I thought how kind he was, and how lucky I was to have him as a doctor. Then I thought I would write to Aunt Margaret without any further delay, and tell her about the baby. I lay back in the long-chair and reflected that it looked as if I would be putting money in the tile factory after all.

Philip had always given me money for housekeeping every month. I had been prepared to keep careful account of this, but he had merely told me to give the ayah what money she said she needed. This went on buying food, and other items for the home. But I could never be sure the ayah was telling the truth about such things. I was pretty certain that she was cheating all the time, as no doubt she had done for years.

Philip bought the drink, and paid the servants. I had nothing to do with that, so really I handled very little money. Philip had never bought me any clothes, although, as I had left England with a good trousseau, I hadn't needed anything. I soon would, of course. I would have to buy what I needed in Madras, with my own money. But it looked as though once again I would be giving my husband money, in spite of the fact that he said I would need it for myself and the baby.

If he were really going to use it to make the factory more efficient, I didn't mind. But the old, nagging doubts came back, although I tried to push them to the back of my mind.

That same week, though, after I had sent a letter home, with news of the forthcoming birth, I received one from my uncle which took me completely by surprise. Aunt Margaret was the one who wrote as a rule; for a moment I feared she might be ill. And then, as I read his letter, I realized that although it was couched in affectionate terms, it was really a business letter. It was to tell me that unfortunately some of my investments were not worth what they had been.

'This is just to let you know that you will be receiving more details later,' ran the letter. 'I am afraid that this means your capital will be considerably less, my dear. I am very sorry about this. I can only say that it is a relief for me to know that all is well with you, and that Philip has a flourishing business'.

I put down the letter and stared in front of me.

'What's wrong?' asked Philip, who

was looking through some correspondence of his own. I handed it to him without speaking. He read it with a look of growing exasperation on his face.

'Well, that's a fine thing!' was his comment. 'It's very strange, Adele. They have looked after your money with remarkable care up to the time of your marriage — now, this! And just at a time when I need all the money I can get — ' He broke off, and threw the letter down.

Uncle Henry's news was a blow to me; it roused feelings of insecurity. It was true that I was still not penniless, but I would no longer have a comfortable private income.

As for Philip and his flourishing business . . . I gave a short, bitter laugh.

'I see nothing to laugh about,' said my husband roughly. 'The Italians will have all my business from me if I don't watch out. I had hoped for some help from you — but now — well, I don't know what we shall do. The baby will be an expense — '

'Yes!' I cried, my voice almost rising to a scream. 'The baby will be an expense — an expense — an expense! What are you going to do about it?'

I could feel myself growing hysterical; I could feel anger suffusing my face with a burning flush. I felt that he should have taken me in his arms, been tender with me; above all, assured me that it did not matter so much. Instead, he had reacted with anger and resentment.

'Oh, stop that noise,' he muttered sullenly. 'I've got enough to think about without you having one of your tantrums — '

'One of *my* tantrums!' I cried. 'You don't say anything about *your* tantrums! You can't rely on money from me in future, that's what it means — and I must say it's strange behaviour from a husband who was surprised to find I had any money at all — '

I broke off at the look on his face. We seemed to be two strangers facing each other, not the couple who had wandered hand in hand in Wales, and loved with such intensity. Why was Philip so different now, and why had everything gone wrong?'

'We'll have to economize in the home,' he said, not taking me up on my last remark. 'There is the baby, of course — '

'*I'll* see the baby has all it needs,' I said angrily. 'You can do without drink for a start, if you want to economize. My baby is going to have everything — and that means I'm going to get an ayah for it, too — '

'An ayah! When we've got an experienced one in the house! There'll be no ayah engaged, you can get that idea out of your head for a start — '

'Oh, yes there will!' I cried. 'And I shall pay her out of my own money — I'm not penniless yet! I'm not having that woman touching my child — I've told you before, we don't need her in the house. I can get a nice girl, Mrs Snow knows one, and she can maid for me, and look after the baby — '

'How dare you discuss our private affairs with Mrs Snow, or any of those women?' he asked, his face white with anger under the tan. 'Don't you ever do it again — ever! You prattle about our business to the gossips of Sadura; you come poking your nose into the tile factory, wanting to know the ins and outs of everything — and your idea of economizing is to get rid of the ayah, who is worth a dozen servants — '

'She may be to you,' I gasped, breathless with anger, 'but not to me! She can go — '

He moved towards me in such a threatening way that I cried out in sudden fear. 'The ayah stays!' he shouted, his face livid, and his hand came down on the side of my face with a sharp smack. For a moment I was rigid with shock; I could not believe that he had struck me. Then a resentment so enormous swept through me that it seemed as if I had not been angry before.

I dashed to the door, and, picking up a porcelain statuette from a carved table, I threw it at him with all the force

I could muster. Whether it hit him or not I didn't wait to see. I heard it shatter to fragments on the tiled floor. Despite the heat I ran upstairs and locked myself in the bedroom. I was laughing as if I would never stop. I knew the statuette of the laughing buddha was valuable — well, it was gone now. That would teach him, I thought. But as I lay on the bed, the laughter turned swiftly to tears. I waited for footsteps on the stairs, but there were none. I began to feel the reaction from the emotions of the past few minutes.

I was shaking, and the perspiration began to roll off me, wave after wave of it, in the sticky heat of that room. How had that angry scene happened? How had it all come about, when all I wanted was to be happy, and to try and make a success of my marriage? But it would not have happened if Philip had taken me in his arms after reading that letter, and had said that it didn't matter all that much, and that we would manage anyway.

It was his behaviour which had triggered off the quarrel. I had intended to mention my ideas concerning engaging a girl for the baby when he was in the right frame of mind, and anyway, not until much later in the year. But I had screamed out everything to him — and angered him still further by letting him know that Mrs Snow had suggested it. And in the end it had boiled down to my dislike and mistrust of the ayah, and his taking her part, as usual.

But whatever the rights and wrongs of it, he had no business to strike me. The thought came to me, as it had come to me so often since I had married Philip — what would my aunt and uncle think if they knew some of the things that went on at Lebanon? Then I thought of Dr Baxter. He had told me to take things as they came, and keep as tranquil as possible. He was always so kind; so understanding. Why couldn't Philip be more like that?

He seemed so selfish, somehow . . .

Thoughts like these kept whirling through my head as I lay there. And the tears went on steadily gushing; whatever my husband's shortcomings, I was married to him, and expecting his child. And the child would have a right to a happy home when it came. As my tears slowly lessened, and I grew calmer, thoughts of England came persistently into my mind. Aunt Margaret's words came back to me, as I had never thought they would: 'If you are not happy there, don't stay'.

Well, I wasn't happy, but happy or not, I would have to live through the next few months, and have my child. Afterwards, perhaps things would be better. Perhaps Philip would change . . . perhaps . . .

I did not see him for the rest of the day. He did not appear at dinner. I had bathed my eyes and appeared outwardly calm, sitting alone while the ayah shuff-shuffed about. I had decided not to stay in the house in any case. I would order the bullock-coach and go for a drive — perhaps on to the ridge. If he came back, he would find me out, and if he didn't, it was better than brooding in the house at all events.

There was a distinct bruise on my cheek; looking in my dressing-table mirror, resentment flared in me again. I dressed my hair forward to conceal the mark. He was not going to treat me in that manner, he would soon find that out. All traces of the laughing buddha had been removed. I wondered grimly if he had told the ayah there had been an accident — no, she had probably heard the whole row, and the crash. After all, she spent a good deal of her time listening at doors.

She knew well enough how I felt towards her, although on the whole her manner towards me was outwardly respectful. She showed her dislike in her insolent smile; in the way she would stop speaking English as soon as Philip appeared, and in other, hardly definable ways.

I ordered the bullock-coach, and drove out on the ridge, getting out at the usual place, and walking along. There were not many people there tonight, no Mrs Radstock, nor the Dysarts to pass the time of day with. Nor was Dr Baxter there. Perhaps he was with someone desperately ill, or perhaps he was dining with the Dysarts — with the very pretty Rosalie. I thought of their charming house, like Lebanon it was an older type of Indian house, set in a pleasant garden.

Dr Baxter lived in the more usual bungalow, with a good cook, and a devoted houseboy. He had entertained us there a couple of times, but there was no doubt that it was lacking a hostess, as Mrs Snow had remarked more than once. Rosalie Dysart would be a lucky girl if she married him, I thought bitterly. I turned round and walked back to the bullock-coach.

Philip did not return that night. I slept little, tormented by the heat, and by worry. Where was he? Was he out drinking — gambling? Wherever he was, he had a right to let me know. How dare he leave me alone in the house to worry like this! But had he come to some harm? Was something wrong?

I lay turning first in one position, and then in another; it was like lying in a hot bath. Oh, this awful climate! This merciless sun, beating down out of skies blue-grey with heat.

And when darkness fell, and the great bats known as 'flying foxes' roused from their sleep and swooped through the trees, pi-dogs howled in the distance, making the night hideous.

10

It was about three weeks after this when Philip announced that he would be going to Hush Hush Valley for several days.

Somehow we had patched over that quarrel without making it up in so many words. Philip had walked into the house the next day without volunteering any information as to where he had been, and I decided not to ask him any questions. We did not mention money, nor the ayah, nor any of the topics about which we had quarrelled, but we no longer shared the great fourposter bed.

Philip had the bed made up in his dressing room, saying that under the circumstances, and with the weather getting hotter and hotter, he thought it was the best plan. In a way it was a relief, as I did not sleep very well in the heat, and

201

in view of my condition, it could well have been out of husbandly consideration for me. Following Dr Baxter's advice, I made a determined effort to be calm and cheerful, and decided that whatever happened, I would make sure that we did not quarrel again like that. Life proceeded in very much the usual way.

I had asked Philip, very reasonably and cheerfully, if he required money to help the tile factory compete against the Italians. He had accepted my offer, saying that one or two of his tile sorters had been approached by Fattorinis, with offers of more money to work for the other firm.

'They are prepared to bribe and cheat and do everything to get my workers — from my agents to the coolies,' he said.

I now had the details of my financial position, and I knew that I was certainly of much more modest means than formerly. Because of Philip's attitude when I had received that first intimation from my uncle, I did not bring up the subject of my money again. Nor did I mention engaging an ayah when the baby was born. There was plenty of time, I told myself. I simply could not face another quarrel with Philip. Once the baby was born, I would be better able to tackle my problems.

So when he said he would be absent for a few days in Hush Hush Valley, I merely accepted it.

'You won't be lonely, will you?' he asked, almost as an afterthought.

'There are plenty of people I can call on,' I said.

'I want to get a few things sorted out at the coffee-garden, Adele,' he went on. 'If I can get all my business affairs in good order before the really hot weather starts, I shall feel easier in my mind.'

'I suppose it's better for you to go now, in that case,' I agreed. 'After the baby comes I would like to see the coffee-garden myself — ' I broke off and thought for the dozenth time how mysterious the Ghat road always looked, with the dark, forest trees, and the overhanging rocks, leading to the still more mysterious Hush Hush Valley. Why did he always make an excuse for me not to go there? At the present time, of course, he was justified in not allowing me to travel along what I knew was a fairly rough road. But I was determined to see Hush Hush Valley and the estate there after the child was born.

'Well, we'll have to see,' he said lightly. 'But not for the time being.'

He went off to Hush Hush Valley early in the morning, while the dew was still on the flowers. He kissed me goodbye; I was still in bed. I'd had a bad night, and felt far from well. But I thought if I mentioned it to Philip, he would think that I was trying to prevent him from going to Hush Hush Valley. I would rest in bed for most of the morning, I decided. There seemed to be an aching in my limbs, and I had a throbbing headache.

As usual, the ayah tapped on my door, to let me know she had prepared the bathroom for me. I told her that I would not be getting up for a while, and asked for some coffee to be brought up.

'Is there anything else, memsahib?' she asked, standing with the tray in her hands.

'Not just now,' I said. She left the room, and I sat drinking my coffee. In spite of the heat, I began to shake. What was wrong with me? I made a determined effort to control myself, but it seemed to have no effect. The coffee spilt as I tried to hold it to my mouth, with my shaking hands. I lay back in bed, and pulled the bed-clothes around me. I must not be ill, I must not be ill, I kept telling myself, but all the time, I knew I was ill.

It had come on so suddenly. Perhaps it would pass, as quickly as it had come. I closed my eyes and willed myself to feel better, willed the shaking to go. But the shaking did not go, it went on and on, and at the same time, I was sure that I was running a temperature.

I would have to get the doctor, or do

something, if it didn't stop. Sick and dizzy, I crawled out of bed, and put on a wrapper. The house was silent as I descended the stairs; at the foot of them I came face to face with the ayah.

'I am ill,' I said, through chattering teeth. 'I can't stop shaking — ' I felt desperate, although the usual dislike of having to tell the ayah anything rose in me. Yet what else could I do?'

'Go ba-ack to be-ed, memsahib,' she said. 'I will bring you something to stop the shaking. You can only sta-ay in bed.'

Wearily I turned round, and dragged my shivering way back to the bedroom. Why did this have to happen when Philip was away? And did the ayah have a cure for it? It was hard to tell. I knew that the natives brewed up their own remedies for various ailments, but I did not know how effective they were. The sleeping draught she had given me had caused me to have terrible nightmares.

Could I trust her? Should I insist on Dr Baxter being sent for? Would the shaking pass off in any case if I stayed in bed? I crept under the mosquito net again, and lay there. If only it had happened yesterday instead of today, Philip would have been at home . . .

After a while, the ayah appeared with a glass of yellowish liquid.

'What is it?' I asked, through chattering teeth.

'It will make you we-ell, memsahib. Drink.'

I shuddered as I drank it — how bitter it was!

'Now re-est. I will come up later,' said the ayah.

She put another blanket on the bed, and left the room. I huddled under the bedclothes, shivering. Perhaps if I could go to sleep again, I would wake up feeling better. Or should I insist on having the doctor? I lay there, shaking and perspiring and dozing.

After what seemed an age, the ayah appeared again, with another drink for me.

'I don't think I am any better,' I said, trying to rouse myself. 'I had better have Dr Baxter.'

'You will be better after this drink — you wi-ill see. Tomorrow, you will be well.'

I hesitated, not sure what to do.

'Ma-any times I have seen people shaking like you. I have cured them.'

Uneasily I drank again. 'If I'm no better tomorrow, I must have the doctor,' I said.

'He is busy at the hospital today,' she said.

My head did not seem clear enough to work out what she meant. Had they tried to get the doctor for me? 'I must have him tomorrow if I am no better,' I repeated. What was wrong with me? Was it anything to worry about? Or would it pass? So many odd ailments seemed to attack people in this climate; they were taken as a matter of course.

I closed my eyes, and I must have slept. It was morning when I awoke, with a cramp-like pain in my stomach. It seemed to twinge right through my back, making me catch my breath. What was wrong with me now? And I was still shaking . . .

I lay there feeling very ill indeed. I must have help! A feeling of panic set in. The sharpness of the pain brought a moan to my lips. Almost at the same time, the door opened, and the ayah stood there. I tried to sit up in bed, and realized then how weak I was.

'You called out, memsahib?'

'Yes — I am ill! You must get the doctor at once! You must send for him — I am in pain!'

'In pain, memsahib? Wha-at pain?'

I struggled between my dislike of the woman, and my feeling of helplessness. 'You must get Dr Baxter — I have pains — don't you understand? And you — ' I broke off, gasping with the pain, 'you must send for the *dorai*.'

'Mu-ust send for the *dorai*?' she repeated softly.

'Do as I say!' I cried, tears of pain and fear forcing their way down my cheeks.

'Ve-ery well, ve-ery well . . . '

Unhurried, she left the room, and I heard her feet shuff-shuffing away. Would she send for the doctor? Would she send for Philip? A fresh spasm of pain broke over me — what had been in that drink she had given me? Had I been poisoned?

I heard voices downstairs then; a rather loud and determined woman's voice, followed by footsteps on the stairs. The next moment the stout and homely figure of Mrs Snow appeared in the room.

'Well, my dear, I heard you were on your own, and I thought I would call — but you are ill!'

'Yes,' I whispered, hardly able to speak for the pain and the violent shaking. 'I am very ill — '

She tore off her big, ugly sunbonnet, and threw it on the couch. 'Ayah!' she shouted, in a voice which seemed to go right through the house. 'Ayah!' Then she came over to the bed, and asked me where the pain was.

'Get Dr Baxter immediately,' she said

angrily, when the ayah appeared. 'Tell him Mrs Snow says it's urgent — ' She lapsed into Telugu, shouting what sounded like a flood of abuse at the other woman. Then she turned to me, the anger on her face changing to gentleness. 'I'll help you — *I'm* here now,' she said.

'You are kind,' I managed to say. Vaguely I realized that she had taken over the house; I could hear her voice giving orders. What was happening? It was a nightmare; I was lying flat now — no, I was lying with my head sloping downwards — what had they done?

Dr Baxter was in the room now. He and Mrs Snow seemed to be working as a team; someone was bathing my hands and face in a cooling lotion; someone was giving me a sip of fiery liquid. I could hear their voices through a blur of pain and shivering.

' — said she had seen it cure the shakes many a time — ' that was Mrs Snow's voice. 'She knew well enough what she was doing — she's got this to answer for — '

'The trouble is, of course, we can't prove anything — you have to prove these things, Mrs Snow ... we'll see what her husband thinks of this day's work — ' That was Dr Baxter's voice.

' ... got a few things to answer for himself. I took pity on the child straight away ... like a lamb to the slaughter ... as for that business over in Hush Hush Valley ... '

'I don't take notice of every rumour I hear in Sadura. People presume too much at times, Mrs Snow ... '

I seemed to be drifting into a state of semi-consciousness. I still heard snatches of what they were saying, before sleep came.

' ... that poor Forrester girl ... the way he brazens things out ... gets away with ... '

' ... not quite that, Mrs Snow ... ' Their voices dropped to whispers.

When I awoke the room was lit by lamplight. Mrs Snow was still there, but Philip was there, too.

'I'll rest on the couch,' Mrs Snow

was saying. 'You go in the dressing room; I'll call you if there is any need. Dr Baxter will be here first thing in the morning — '

'Philip, I can't stop shivering,' I said. How hoarse and weak my voice sounded. They both came to the bedside. Philip looked strained and frightened. He took my hand in his.

'You are going to get better, Adele,' he said. 'If I had known you were feeling unwell I wouldn't have gone to Hush Hush Valley. Mrs Snow has been very kind, and she is going to stay the night.'

'It came on so suddenly,' I said.

'Yes, it does,' said Mrs Snow soothingly.

'But what is wrong with me?' I asked.

'You've got yourself a dose of malaria, young lady,' said Mrs Snow.

'Malaria?' I said. 'But those pains — '

'Go to sleep again. Dr Baxter will see you in the morning.'

I drifted off to sleep, waking in fits and starts throughout the night. Every time I woke, Mrs Snow was there to attend to me. When morning came, I was still ill and shivering, and very weak.

'Mrs Snow,' I said. 'The baby — ' I couldn't go on.

She took both my hands in hers. 'I'm afraid you've lost it this time,' she said gently. 'I'm so sorry, my dear. I did my best, and so did Dr Baxter. But try not to fret too much. It will take a long time for you to regain your strength.' I turned my face on the pillow, and wept.

During the next few days Philip was in the room a good deal, usually sitting on the couch. Dr Baxter came and went, always kind and gentle. The shaking had left me, except for a recurring spasm. Mrs Snow was still caring for me; the ayah fetched and carried, but did not stay in the room. Sometimes Philip would sit and hold my hand without speaking.

'I'm not having a baby any more,' I said, when he did this once.

'I know, dear. But you are going to

get well. That's all that matters.'

I wondered how deeply Philip had been affected by my illness. Would he change now? I was so depressed at the time that I didn't feel as if I cared one way or the other. One thing seemed to dominate my thoughts; I had been going to have a baby, and now I was not. And somehow, I felt the ayah was responsible.

I remembered the bitter drink she had given me, and how she had seemed loath to send for the doctor until Mrs Snow had arrived. Mrs Snow, with her plain face, and kind heart. I would never be able to thank her enough, nor Dr Baxter, for that matter.

At last I was able to get up and sit on the couch for a while. Philip would sit fanning me with an ostrich feather fan which had belonged to his mother. He had written to my aunt and uncle, telling them of my illness, but had said that I was recovering, and would write to them.

His manner towards me was kind

and considerate, and he was always sober. But I was no longer going to have a child.

'The ayah gave me something to drink which she said would stop the shivering,' I said. 'It was what she gave me that made me lose the baby.'

'Adele, dearest! It was inevitable that it would happen — Dr Baxter will tell you. The ayah gave you what she thought was the remedy, and probably you would have been all right if it had only been malaria. It was the combination of the two that made things so bad — '

'I don't believe it,' I said flatly. 'You refuse to face the truth about the ayah. She has never wanted me here from the start — and if it hadn't been for Mrs Snow, I probably wouldn't be here.'

'You must put these thoughts out of your head. Dearest, I know you are depressed and miserable, it's only natural. But Dr Baxter says he's going to give you a really good tonic — '

He broke off, and fanned me

vigorously. I could see he was not prepared to accept that the ayah had anything to do with my losing the child.

The next few weeks passed slowly, but I was gradually recovering my health. Philip was still tender and thoughtful; he seldom left the house for long. I began to have visitors.

'It must be an awful disappointment,' said Mrs Radstock.

'I'm getting over it, now,' I said. I knew that I would have to get over it.

I made up my mind that as soon as I was fully recovered, I was going to have a say in what went on at the tile factory. I would help out financially if necessary, but I would make suggestions, too. Philip seemed to be in a more reasonable frame of mind altogether. Undoubtedly, he had been very shaken by my illness. Although I knew that I could never recapture my first, ecstatic feelings for him again, I still cared for him. Perhaps this shared sorrow would mark a turning point in our marriage.

Gradually life began to get back to normal.

'I think my calls can cease now, Mrs Belvedere,' said Dr Baxter one day. 'Professionally, I mean.'

'Not in any other way, I hope,' I said with a smile.

'No, not socially. But you are well enough now, provided you take things easy for a while.'

'There is something I would like to know,' I said slowly. 'What was that stuff the ayah gave me to drink? I'm sure it made me lose my baby.'

He seemed to hesitate before replying. 'I asked her what she had given you, and if what she said was true, then it was a perfectly harmless concoction. It might not have done your malaria any good, but it couldn't do any harm.'

I looked at him, and realized that whatever I suspected, I could prove nothing.

'If what she said was true,' I repeated.

'Precisely.' There was compassion and understanding in his blue eyes.

Whatever she had given me to drink, I had drunk, and there was no proof what it was. She could tell the doctor anything. And as she was cunning, she would know of half a dozen other native remedies which were harmless.

I walked out on to the verandah with him. The heat was appalling.

'Are you thinking of going to the Hills for a while?' he asked.

'I don't know — we haven't talked about it yet,' I said.

'Well, you can think about it, I suppose. It's a heat trap here, but there's always a breeze on the ridge. And one other thing, Mrs Belvedere — '

'Yes?'

'It's natural for you and your husband to long for a child to replace the one you have lost. But it would not be wise for you to start a family again too soon — not this year, anyway.'

'I see.'

He put on his wide-brimmed hat, and I waved him off from the verandah.

I went back into the house. I knew that I had to do something before I could put things out of my mind, and make a fresh start. I went into the drawing room, and opened the beautiful, carved work-box, which had belonged to Philip's mother.

Inside were the tiny, filmy garments which I had worked upon day after day. For one brief moment my eyes filled with tears.

I picked up one little gown, so daintily tucked and trimmed with lace, and clasped it to me. How empty it was. Then I went upstairs to my dressing room. It had a cupboard which was to have been my baby's; already there were sundry articles inside. I would put these garments in, and close the door on a sad episode in my life. There were about half a dozen books belonging to Philip pushed away inside. They might as well stay there, I thought. On an impulse I picked one up, and turned over the pages cursorily. To my surprise, there was a folded letter inside. It was not in an envelope. I unfolded it, and the words seemed to leap out of the pages at me.

'My darling Philip,' it ran — 'my parents are doing everything in their power to make me leave Sadura; they are even suggesting that I go back to England for a while. They are making my life a misery, but it makes no difference to my love for you. They are prejudiced against you; when I ask them why they don't approve of you, they just say you have a bad reputation. I have pointed out that before I came to Sadura they attended social functions where you were present, and that they never said anything about your reputation until they knew that we were interested in each other.

'They said that was because it had never affected them until I came to live with them, and that here in Sadura Europeans stuck together in a way which is not necessary back home. They say that certain 'practices' are tolerated here, but they won't say what these practices are. They merely say that they will not permit me to form an attachment with you, because you are most unsuitable. My darling, they do not understand how much I love you! They have no idea how happy we are in each other's company. I wish I could be clasped in your arms now. You make me feel so loved and cherished. They have forbidden me to see you again, but I shall do so at every opportunity. I am your true wife, in everything but name . . .'

There was more in the same vein, and the letter was signed 'Your ever loving Dorothy'. The address was in Sadura, and the date was nearly a year before I met Philip in London. I read it again, and then replaced it in the book. I was trembling all over. Dorothy! I *knew* that letter had been written by Dorothy Forrester, the girl who had committed suicide. I walked into my bedroom and sat down on the couch. This was the scandal that I had heard vaguely hinted at.

I remembered what Philip had said when I had mentioned her once. 'Rather a silly, hysterical type of girl.' Thus he had dismissed her. The realization of the whole tragedy seemed to seep slowly into me as I sat there. She had been madly in love with him, there was no doubt about that. And her parents had not approved . . .

I thought of the poignant sentence: 'I am your true wife in everything but name'. The meaning of that was plain enough. I was a bit more worldly wise than when Philip had first met me. It was true about the English in Sadura sticking together. Mrs Snow had once told me that on the whole, people were more tolerant of a lot of things out in India. She said people got away with behaviour which would keep them out of most respectable houses in England. But she had not enlarged on that.

Whatever Philip had done in the past, he was still more or less accepted in Sadura society. We received invitations, and entertained. When we had given that first dinner party, Philip had said that he wanted to show me off, that he wanted to show them all at Sadura what he had brought back from home. Why had he left Sadura for a stay in England, though, at that particular time? When had Dorothy Forrester taken her life — and why? Question after question crowded in on me as I sat there.

What were these 'practices' that were tolerated in Sadura? I felt dazed, as though these things were happening to somebody else, not to me. But the question which seemed to override all other questions was how many more shocks was I going to have concerning Philip? Was there no end to my disillusionment and unhappiness? Just as I was putting away the unwanted baby clothes to make a fresh start, I had to be confronted by this ugliness from the past. But still, I told myself, it *was* the past. Perhaps Philip had been a bit wild; had trifled with the girl's affections — not taken her as seriously as she had taken him.

For a long time I sat there, thinking about it. I wished with all my heart that I had not found that letter. After all, it had been in the pages of that book all this time. Finding it and reading it hadn't altered anything.

Shuff-shuff, shuff-shuff — the ayah's footsteps outside the door. She tapped on it softly. 'Are you there, memsahib?'

'Yes. What is it?'

She opened the door a few inches. 'The *dorai* is back, and asked me to see where you were. He wishes to take tea.'

'I shall be coming down directly,' I said coldly. I glanced at myself in the mirror, and combed up a stray lock of hair. If only it wasn't so hot! The slightest movement was an effort. I went slowly downstairs and into the drawing room.

Philip came up to me and kissed me. 'What did the doctor say?' he asked.

'I'm better,' I said. 'He's not coming visiting me again, not professionally, anyway.'

He clasped me in his arms and swung me round, as he had not done for a long time.

'Philip!' I protested, but I was laughing.

'I'm so glad, dearest. It's been a bad year for us up to now, but we'll make up for it, you'll see. We'll have a celebration dinner with Mrs Snow and Dr Baxter as guests of honour.'

'That would be nice,' I said.

'We'll make a fresh start, Adele.'

We sat side by side on the couch, and Philip put his arm around me. The punkah swung to and fro, and his beautiful mother gazed down at us from the wall. I told myself that the letter I had found by accident belonged to the past. He was my husband, and he wanted us to make a fresh start. I must go forward, not brood about things which were over and done with.

'We've been apart for so long with one thing and another, I haven't felt as though I've had a wife,' he murmured.

He drew me close to him, and once

226

again, my fears over so many things were stifled, or nearly so. Perhaps my illness and danger had brought him to his senses as nothing else could have.

As he remarked, it had been a bad year for us up to then. My financial losses, the Italian competition, my illness and the loss of the baby — not to mention that terrible quarrel when he had slapped me, and I had smashed the laughing buddha . . .

'Things will be better from now on, Adele,' he said.

11

'To Mrs Snow and Dr Baxter,' said Philip. We stood up and drank a toast. Mr Snow glanced with fond pride at his plump and much loved wife. For much loved she was in Sadura, and now I knew why.

Rosalie Dysart dimpled prettily, her eyes on David Baxter. There was no doubt in my mind that she wanted him. She had told me that she thought he worked too hard sometimes.

'He goes over to that awful hospital, and attends to people there, as well as his other patients,' she had told me. 'He puts his work before everything.'

Even before you, I thought. Aloud I said, '*I'm* very glad he does, for one.'

Rosalie laughed. 'Oh, well,' she said. 'I understand how you must feel — I would, if I'd been ill. But sometimes he has to break social engagements because of patients. It's rather annoying when it happens.'

I knew that she meant it was rather annoying for her, and disappointing, too, I had no doubt. Just the same, I wondered if she was building up her hopes too high. They may whisper about her in the bazaar, and say that she wanted the young doctor, but that did not mean that he wanted her. But why was I thinking like this? What did it matter to me? I had my own husband, and since I had recovered from my illness, I really felt that things were going to be better. Philip said that he had increased the pay of some of the best workers in the factory, and he thought we were holding our own with the Italians.

So I tried to put behind me the memory of my husband's drinking, lies, and duplicity. I tried not to think about the letter from that dead girl; not to wonder what those 'practices' were which were tolerated in Sadura.

This was our celebration dinner, and

everyone seemed in good spirits. The usual people were gathered in our dining room; the Dysarts, the Radstocks, the Walkers, and several other couples, most of them long standing residents of Sadura.

'They say there's going to be a devil-dance up on the ridge,' remarked Mrs Walker, sipping her wine appreciatively. 'I've never seen one.'

'What are they like?' asked Miss Dysart. 'I would love to see one.'

'Would you really?' My husband sounded rather surprised. 'I heard from the ayah that they were having one — of course, her brother, old Chitteranjan is the devil-dancer.'

'He must have some energy, then, if he's going to dance tonight,' remarked Mr Snow. 'He's been at it ever since I can remember. When does a devil-dancer retire? And who takes his place?'

'It's a highly skilled occupation,' said Philip. 'I suppose there must be somebody ready to step into his shoes — if he wore shoes, that is.'

'I would still love to see him,' persisted Rosalie. She glanced at Dr Baxter. 'Wouldn't you?' she asked. Then she turned to me. 'Wouldn't you?'

There was a short, slightly uncomfortable silence.

'You do have some odd ideas, Rosalie,' said her mother.

'Well . . . ' I said, looking at Philip.

'I leave it to our guests,' he said smoothly. 'We can either stay here and amuse ourselves, or get into the bullock-coaches, and visit the devil-shrine on the ridge. It's not considered a spectacle for white people as a rule, but certainly they would not try to prevent anyone from this house from watching. The ayah is not going; I suppose she has seen so many *nemas*.'

Rosalie looked quite excited. 'Oh, let's go, then,' she said. I caught Dr Baxter's eye. A vague apprehension stirred in me.

'Mrs Belvedere looks a bit frightened,' he said, as though he had sensed my reluctance.

Rosalie turned to me. 'You're not, are you?'

'Not really. We'll go, if everyone is in agreement.'

Some time later we took to the bullock-coaches, and drove up on to the ridge. It was a windless, choking night. The grass was burnt brown, the earth black. It seemed as though everything was waiting for the monsoon. Philip had told me that throughout the weeks of rain to come, not a tile could be shipped away; it was impossible for a boat to get up the river. He had been to Hush Hush Valley again, and brought little Hanna back for another stay. Once again she was around the house. A strange pang stirred in me when I saw Philip playing with her one day. I could not dislike the little girl, she was so sweet, even if she was the ayah's grandchild.

Anyway, she would be going back soon, she would have to go before the rains came. That meant Philip would have to make another journey to Hush

Hush Valley. I had made up my mind that I was going to see that place after the monsoon. So many things were going to be done after the monsoon; Philip had even mentioned having trolley rails installed at the tile works.

Dr Baxter moved in beside me as we began to walk along in a group. 'You are looking quite well, now,' he remarked. 'I hope you are not going to get upset at the sight of old Chitteranjan dancing around in his warpaint. The plain fact of the matter is that we are really all coming to humour Miss Dysart.'

'I know,' I replied with a smile.

Philip walked ahead, leading the party, talking to Mr Radstock, followed by the Dysarts. Rosalie dropped back, and began to walk on the other side of Dr Baxter. Did he care for her, I wondered, for the hundredth time. Mrs Snow had once talked to me of the wife he had lost so early in his married life.

'She was not beautiful, at all,' she said. 'But she was very kind, and unselfish. She was also very brave. I was with her at the end.'

Her words came back to me as we walked along the ridge, with Rosalie chattering away vivaciously to both of us. Soon we were nearly up to the big trees, and the devil-shrine. It was alive with activity, something which I had never seen before.

'We won't be going inside the enclosure, will we?' asked Rosalie, rather nervously.

'We certainly won't — we'll see all we want to from outside the walls,' said Philip. 'I think you're beginning to get a bit frightened, Miss Dysart,' he added, with a rather mischievous smile.

'Indeed I'm not,' she declared.

I said nothing, because I felt a pang of fear myself as we drew closer.

Bamboo torches set in barrels were lit all round the inside of the enclosure, and people were squatting around, smoking or chewing betel, and talking to each other. At the far end of the enclosure a tent was rigged up, and several men were sitting outside with tom-toms. Undoubtedly it was from here that the devil-dancer would emerge. The torches flickered; there was an air of concentrated expectancy from the audience.

A shudder ran right through me. Then, suddenly, a figure emerged from the tent, a figure with a sword, leaping about, rattling a bell, but it was not Chitteranjan.

'Oh . . . ' gasped Rosalie.

'That's the *pujari,* not the devil-dancer,' explained Philip. 'This fellow is just to get the audience in the right mood.'

'Are you ladies still sure that you want to stay?' enquired Dr Baxter.

'Yes,' said Rosalie, both fear and fascination in her voice.

'We may as well see the show through,' said Mrs Walker. 'I was the one who mentioned it in the first place. Anyway, it's an experience.'

She was right about that. Standing there, watching the silent, squatting crowd, and the shouting, leaping figure doing his strange dance, a curious, unexpected excitement rose in me. He disappeared into the tent as quickly as he had come. We waited breathlessly, then, moving slowly, Chitteranjan, the devil-dancer, emerged. Naked except for a loin cloth, he moved forward on stick-like legs, mouthing hideous animal noises. His face was painted yellow, and he wore a head-dress of coconut leaves. Immediately he appeared there was a great roll from the tom-toms.

Then he began to leap about, faster and faster. The motionless spectators took up a curious wailing, and the torches flickered. Faster and faster the man danced, his eyes blank, his mouth shouting unintelligibly. The sweat ran from him, smearing the paint daubs on his chest.

'Why,' I said, half to myself, 'he's possessed.'

'He's drugged,' said Dr Baxter briefly.

A strange terror and mingled fascination took hold of me. I was both thrilled and frightened; nothing could have made me leave that bizarre scene. That dreadful, wailing cry, that grotesque figure dancing and contorting itself; the flickering torches and the throbbing tomtoms seemed to stir something savage and primitive inside me. Then, suddenly, Chitteranjan stopped dancing, and at the same time the tom-toms stopped too. For a moment he stood motionless, then he began to walk round the crowd, picking out individuals and talking to them in a voice that was like no voice I had ever heard. It was horrible, sinister; more frightening even than the dance itself. Droning and inhuman, the voice went on, the claw-like hand raised, pointing at first one and then the other. He moved steadily round the crowd.

'Death and destruction,' whispered Dr Baxter, a glint of amusement in his eye. 'Half of them won't sleep tonight — and when they do, they'll be agreeably surprised to find themselves wake up in the morning.'

Relentlessly Chitteranjan picked out his victims. He was not speaking English, but he seemed to be repeating the same words over and over again.

'What is he saying?' I asked.

'He's a jolly little fellow, as I've told you before. He's forecasting death — in very liberal doses, too. He's bound to be right eventually, of course.'

In spite of Dr Baxter's lighthearted words, I felt a pang of fear. It was sinister, horrible! Then Chitteranjan caught sight of us, and began to make his way determinedly forward. I wanted to go, and yet I was rooted to the spot. That dreadful face and voice; instinctively I stepped back a pace or two, as he reached the wall.

The scrawny hand pointed forward — straight at Philip! I gave a gasp of fear, as a meaningless jabber of words poured out. I moved nearer to Philip, and took his arm. That ochre-stained face with the staring eyes and lipless mouth; that emaciated body and pointing finger — it was too much.

'Go away!' I cried. Rather to my surprise, he did. It was like a spell being broken.

'Come on, we've seen enough,' said Mrs Snow, before anyone else spoke. The men of the party agreed immediately, with the exception of Philip, who did not speak.

We moved away with a feeling of relief, while Dr Baxter talked quite cheerfully about the devil-dancing, and what an old rogue the ayah's brother was. But neither his cheerfulness not his reassuring smile made any difference to my feelings. He had already told me what Chitteranjan was saying to his victims as he picked them out. And he had said it to Philip; pointed and repeated it over and over again. Death . . .

'He was horrible,' I said, when we were in the bullock-coach. 'I wish we hadn't come.'

'He's not to be taken seriously, Adele. I'm hardly likely to be frightened by an ignorant old man like that, am I? Anyway, according to him, when the monsoon comes, we will all be winnowed out. He, I suppose, will be among the chosen few who survive — presumably to carry on his devil-dancing. I must say, though, I didn't think he would have the impertinence to address any of his idiotic remarks to me.'

With that he apparently dismissed the subject. I could not, though, and long after Philip slept, I lay awake, still seeing that hideous face, and hearing that droning voice.

12

The following morning, Philip announced that he was going to Hush Hush Valley again.

'I suppose you are taking Hanna back before the rains start,' I said.

'Er — no, I'm not taking Hanna this time.' He looked at his coffee cup with great interest. 'The monsoon won't break for another ten days or so. I have to go, but the ayah wants her granddaughter to stay for a few more days. I've time to pay two visits to Hush Hush Valley before the rains start. I shall be staying with an old planter friend, Cyril Hauser. He's been away for several months.'

'I don't see how you can be so sure the rains won't start for another ten days,' I said. 'It sounds as if you are making two journeys when only one would be necessary. If the monsoon begins early, you'll be marooned over in Hush Hush Valley.'

'Adele, dear, what do you know of monsoons?' There was an edge of impatience to his voice. Then he reached out and squeezed my hand placatingly.

'Oh, very well,' I said. 'And don't forget, I'm coming to see the coffee-garden for myself when the monsoon is over.'

'Of course you are,' he said lightly.

After Philip had kissed me goodbye, and I had waved to him from the verandah, I went back in the house to write some letters. Social life at Sadura was rather disrupted now, as some of the wives had gone to the Hills. Mrs Radstock was in a bungalow there; Philip had asked me if I wanted to go, too, and I had decided against it. I didn't want us to be separated when it seemed things were going to be so much better.

As I sat at the writing desk, a sudden sound made me jump. A child laughed;

I turned round to see Hanna standing in the room, wearing a gaudy, pink dress. Her enormous eyes looked up into mine, and she smiled disarmingly, showing her little white teeth. She was plumper than most Indian children of her age; a very pretty child indeed.

'Helloa,' I said, smiling back, torn between my dislike of the ayah, and the charm of this child.

'Hel-loa,' she replied slowly, her eyes unwavering. So she spoke the odd word of English. Well, no doubt the ayah's daughter spoke it when necessary. I picked up a china dish of bon-bons, and offered her one.

'Thank you,' I said encouragingly.

'Tha-ang,' she said, with a little giggle, taking one.

I laughed too; I couldn't help it.

'Wa-alk,' she said, and reaching out her hand, clasped mine. For a moment I hesitated. The ayah was busy, no doubt. A walk — why not? I picked up my sunbonnet, and put it on.

There were great wads of flowers in

Hanna's hair; the perfume from them mingled with the smell of coconut oil, with which her locks were heavily anointed. The bangles which she wore, and the heavy earrings which swung when she moved her head, were somehow incongruous on so young a child. Not to an Indian, though, I reflected, as we walked out on to the verandah together. In a couple of hours the heat would be unbearable; I would be lying down with the punkah swishing to and fro. Although I hadn't really raised any objections about Philip going to Hush Hush Valley, I felt myself wishing that he hadn't gone.

We walked into the parched brown of the garden. How strange this dry, charred, grass appeared after the green lushness of Wiltshire.

'Where are we going?' I asked Hanna. She shook her head and smiled. We went past the queer, tiny servants huts, and over the hard ground. Then I realized where she was taking me; she wanted to show me her grandmother's house. Although situated more privately than the others, it was much the same. Hanna led me inside, and said something, but not in English. The floor looked exactly like black marble, but I knew that it was not. I had seen floors like this before, but Philip had told me it was a mixture of cow-dung and lamp-black, and a good deal of elbow grease.

The ayah's house boasted three rooms, though, unlike most comparable hovels. She had a table and four cane-bottom chairs in the room we entered, also an old couch. On the walls hung bazaar oddments, lucky charms, carvings of various gods, and, rather incongruously, a few crude paintings of saints. The bedroom into which Hanna led me was sparsely furnished, a low bed with a blanket thrown across, a chest of drawers, and more paintings and gimcrack ornaments. Behind this room was a tiny bathing room.

It was, I suppose, pretty well what I might have expected. I might have expected, too, the mingled smell of incense and cashew-arrack that lingered around the place. Despite the fact that the ayah's house appeared poor, I knew by now that the Indians were a thrifty race with a high regard for money. She would have a nest-egg put away somewhere. What caught my eye, though, was a framed photograph on the chest of drawers. It was a very carefully posed picture of a beautiful Indian girl holding a baby a few months old. Undoubtedly it must be the ayah's daughter, with Hanna as a baby.

'Your mama?' I asked. She nodded solemnly, although I could not be sure that she understood what I said. 'Are we going back, then?' was my next question. I moved towards the door, and she seemed quite ready to go, having shown me the ayah's house.

I reflected as we walked back that she could wander at will in our large garden, and be safe enough. As I was thinking this, with Hanna trotting along beside me, I noticed that big clouds seemed to be sweeping in from the sea. They were black and lowering. Where had the sun gone? The ayah was out on the verandah as we approached the house. Hanna let go my hand, and ran forward to her grandmother, chattering. Obviously she was telling her where we had been, but the ayah appeared not to be taking much notice.

'The monsoon is coming early, memsahib,' she said.

'But it can't come yet . . . ' I looked up at the sky, dark and ominous. 'I thought people here could time it almost to the day.'

'It is ready,' said the ayah heavily. 'It is co-oming early. I can tell.'

'But Mr Belvedere will be in Hush Hush Valley,' I exclaimed. 'What will he do?'

The ayah shook her head. 'The *dorai* will not come through the monsoon — he could not travel the Ghat road. Besides, they sa-ay it will be very bad this year.'

'They say!' I cried. 'Who says?' But I

247

didn't wait for her to answer. I went into the house, and left the ayah and Hanna both staring after me. Even if it did come early, I thought, that didn't mean it would come today — or tomorrow. And Philip was coming back tomorrow. He would make an early start back. He would certainly not get caught in the monsoon.

Even as I reasoned this, I felt uneasy fear rise in me. Suppose it was a bad monsoon, and Philip got cut off in Hush Hush Valley? In that case, he would be cut off for weeks. I thought of the dark, looming Ghats, and pictured them in the full blast of the monsoon's fury. I knew from what Philip had said, that, however bad the monsoon was here, it was always worse on the Ghats; to every three inches of rain we got, they would get six.

I sat thinking about this, listening to the faint, recurring squeak of the punkah ropes. As the day advanced, a mist began to come down. It seemed dark everywhere. There was a quick shower.

'It's just a shower,' I told the ayah. 'It should brighten up now.'

'It wo-on't brighten up, memsahib,' she said quietly, and shuff-shuffed out of the room.

I was afraid, but I would not show it. I thought of her brother, the devil-dancer, and his prophecy of terrible floods. I thought, too, of his claw-like hand pointing at Philip, and that hideous yellow face with its lipless mouth talking of death. I wrote some more letters, and tried to read. Then I went out on to the verandah again, to find that a wind had sprung up. It would blow those dark clouds away, I thought. Slowly the day dragged on. I toyed with the idea of visiting somebody, but restless though I felt in the house, I was reluctant to leave it. At last, night fell, still with the sound of the wind sighing.

It took me a long time to get to sleep, and when I did I was awakened by a howling gale which seemed to be shaking the house to its very foundations,

249

and mingled with that was the sound of torrential rain.

I lay in bed, silent, terrified. The ayah had been right. The monsoon had come. As the greyness of dawn began to lighten the room, I crept to the window. I had never imagined anything as frightening as this. Everywhere seemed to be a dark, solid sheet of water. The zinc spouts in the roof were shooting out great rivers of rain, mingling with the downpour. Huge dark clouds seemed to be pressing down on the very house itself; the thought came to me, thank goodness we are not in a valley, to be followed immediately by the thought that Philip was. I went back to bed, and lay there trembling, for what seemed like hours.

For once I was glad to hear the shuff-shuff of the ayah's feet, and her reassuring tap on the door. I had been considering going down to see if Babwah was aroused. The morning routine of toilette and break-fast gave things a temporary illusion of normality, but I could tell from the excited chatter of the servants that the monsoon was making itself felt. Although the dislike between myself and the ayah was mutual, she did volunteer some information when she served me with breakfast.

She told me that a number of mud huts by the creek had been washed away in the night; there had been a landslide blocking the road; the hills were just like a sheet of falling water.

'What will it be like at Hush Hush Valley — ' I began, and stopped as I saw fear on the ayah's face. And then I felt fear too, welling up inside me. The sight of food made me feel sick.

'The bungalow Sajoodaye li-ive in over at Hush Hush Valley — I am afraid — ' she wailed.

'What about my husband?' I cried. 'Oh . . . Philip!' Little Hanna ran into the room, and regarded us both with dark, frightened eyes. The thunderous rain and wind had upset her, but even more so the sight of fear in the grown-ups around her. She began to whimper. For a brief moment the ayah and I were united in anxiety; she mainly for her daughter, Sajoodaye, and I for my husband. Why, oh why had he gone to that wretched coffee-garden over at Hush Hush Valley, when the monsoon was on the point of breaking? He had said it would be another ten days before it broke.

'Perhaps things will not be as bad as we think, over at Hush Hush Valley,' I said, as much to comfort myself as the ayah.

'Other years the-ey not too bad,' she said. 'This time, ve-ery bad monsoon — bad now, worse to come. My brother tell true, and he to-old me.'

I shuddered. That corpse-like face, talking of death! Oh, Philip! Philip! I sent up a silent prayer for his safety. As long as he was safe, I didn't mind if he stayed at Hush Hush Valley for the next few weeks, until the Ghat road was passable again. As long as he was safe — but he must be safe! He must be! For the next hour my thoughts ran round in circles; outside, the fury of the monsoon continued. Then, unannounced and unceremoniously, the dripping figure of Ernest Jones appeared in the gloom of the drawing room.

'Mrs Belvedere, the river is rising. The last *pattimar* with the last load of tiles left yesterday — ' He broke off, his face anxious. Our eyes met. He knew that Philip was away, and he had come to me.

'Well — ' I was at a loss. 'What do you do other years when the monsoon comes?' I asked, trying to sound calm.

'Other years not so bad as this. The river has been rising for a day and a night — it's into the office now. The whole place is shaking, everyone has left. The accounts — the cash box — '

Suddenly I knew what had to be done. 'You want them transferred here?' I asked.

He nodded. 'I must have help.'

'I'll help you,' I said. 'And we'll take one of the houseboys.'

'I cannot ask you to come out in this, Mrs Belvedere.'

'I'm coming,' I said calmly. 'It's only rain.'

I summoned Babwah, and told him he was to accompany us to the factory. He rolled his eyes, and produced an enormous black umbrella. He also draped a dun-coloured blanket round himself. Meanwhile I put on some boots, and buttoned myself into Philip's oilskins. They were far too big, but better than nothing.

The three of us set off from the house, Babwah holding the umbrella somewhat precariously over me.

'It's no use bringing that, it will blow inside out,' I said, rather crossly. Seconds later it did; Babwah gave a despairing howl, and let it go. It was difficult to walk in the teeth of that wind; a wind that was packed with solid, driving water.

'If I may suggest it, we would do better arm in arm,' said Ernest Jones anxiously. 'If you would come in the middle, Mrs Belvedere — '

I took up his suggestion, and the

three of us struggled along in this manner. We did not speak; I was gasping with the strain. I could hear Babwah's teeth chattering, and his breath coming in sobs.

We slithered on the wet slopes of the hill, and then I caught sight of the Gawari, dark grey, menacing, and moving with an ominous swiftness. Approaching the factory, we were now walking through a couple of inches of flood water. The rain seemed to be bursting on us like waves. On, on we went, until we stood at last in the office of the building. For a moment I leaned against the wall, exhausted. The place was deserted, but outside, the fury of the gale went on unabated. There was water on the floor, spreading rapidly.

'No time to lose,' said Ernest warningly. He began to put papers into files.

'How are we going to carry all the books and things?' I asked dubiously.

'In a sack. I have one here.'

I recovered somewhat from the

ordeal of battling with the monsoon, and systematically began to turn out drawers and collect files. We worked together, going through papers, old receipts, bills — yes, there were plenty of those, I noticed. I also found the title deeds for Lebanon, and for the estate at Hush Hush Valley. Even in the midst of the confusion, and my worry about Philip, I felt exasperated that he had kept important documents in the office at the works. They should have been kept in the house. We had Babwah putting everything in the sack, but it soon became obvious that there was too much for one sack.

'We'd better get the cash box in,' I said.

Ernest straightened up. 'We'll have to make another journey, I'm afraid.'

The same thought had occurred to me.

'If we have to, we have to,' I said.

'Perhaps you need not come, Mrs Belvedere.'

'I shall come. It's my place to come

when Mr Belvedere is away.'

Ernest roped up the sack, tying the front part round his own body. 'The three of us will have to carry it — it's easier that way,' he said. 'Your best position is probably in the middle, Mrs Belvedere.'

Babwah seemed quite beyond speech. We set out into the teeth of the monsoon again. I could feel my boots squelching with every step, as we somehow rounded the hill, and made our way back to the house.

'Mr Jones will stay for tiffin,' I instructed the ayah. 'We are having to go back to the factory again.' Babwah looked so completely beaten down with misery that I had a wild impulse to laugh. I had heard people described as wet blankets, but I had never seen anyone who so fitted the description as he did. He dripped all over the place.

'You can't get any wetter,' I said consolingly.

The second time we set out from the house was even worse. If anything, it seemed as if the fury of the monsoon was increasing. And once we had rounded the brow of the hill, and looked into the creek, I saw that the flood waters were raging onwards, unabated. They were moving now with a swirling motion; the river had turned into a terrifying sea, surging steadily forward under a black sky. If it was like this here — Oh, God, I thought, what must it be like in Hush Hush Valley?

There were four inches of water now in the office.

'It's going to be flooded!' I cried, as though I had not believed it before. Ernest Jones produced another sack, and we filled it hurriedly. I remained outwardly calm, but I could feel the place shaking. Babwah stumbled round in a daze, his face a mask of fear and misery, as though wondering how much more he would have to endure at our hands.

At last we filled the second sack, and Ernest roped it up as with the first. Anything that was left of use, he had put on the high shelves. No man could have done more, I thought, watching him. At the same time came the bitter thought that there was no sign of the foreman, Bango. We had no time to lose, the river was rising every minute. Outside, I gave an involuntary cry of fear; we were almost wading through flood water now. It was terrifying beyond anything I had imagined; a sinister grey tide of water, sucking, swirling, rain-lashed water.

Somehow, the three of us stumbled along, Ernest leading, with the sack tied round his waist, and one arm round it, with me in the middle, holding it so tightly that my arm was numb. Babwah brought up the rear, whining to himself, but holding on to the sack, nevertheless. In this manner, we proceeded back, and at long last the waterlogged steps up to the verandah at Lebanon rose in front of us. Whatever happened to the factory now, at least the ledgers, the papers, the files and the money were safe.

13

The monsoon raged on. The river rose and rose, and swept away all before it, a mass of swirling, greedy water. I knew that the factory was completely flooded, that people were fleeing for safety, or being drowned, and that the Ghat road was impassable.

No official news came from Hush Hush Valley, just frightening little snippets; the valley was under water; drowned bodies were being washed up everywhere. But Philip would be safe — he must be safe, I told myself desperately. A kind of resolute cheerfulness made me carry on. I kept myself as busy as possible, sorting through all the factory papers. I simply would not let myself think Philip could be anything but safe.

I knew that the ayah was suffering. She went about her duties as usual;

when she left the house she wrapped a blanket around herself and Hanna. Strangely enough, Hanna became a comfort to me as well as her grandmother during our shared anxiety. She could not play in the garden now, so she sat with me quite often, nursing a doll, and repeating English words after me. She could well be an orphan without knowing it, I thought, and straight away put the idea out of my mind.

At night, though, when I lay alone in that great bed, I could not control my fears. If only the rain would stop — if only it would stop just for a few days — just long enough for me to make some kind of contact with the outside world. For my world had shrunk now; I was confined to Lebanon, to reading, to playing with Hanna, and to wondering about Philip.

I did have one visitor, though. Dr Baxter was on the doorstep the first day that the monsoon eased slightly. Having kept up an appearance of cheerfulness in front of the servants, I burst into tears as soon as he stepped into the drawing room.

'Well — Mrs Belvedere!'

'I can't help it,' I sobbed. 'I'm sorry to greet you like this, but I'm trapped in the house, and my husband is trapped over at Hush Hush Valley — '

'Yes, I heard he was there.' His face was grave.

'Have you heard anything? Is there any news — ?' My voice died away.

'There is no official news at all yet. Things are pretty difficult, as you can imagine. As a rule, there isn't much a bullock-coach can't get through, but the monsoon is exceptional this year. I hear the factory is flooded.'

'Yes. But I went out with the chief clerk, and we brought all the ledgers and things back here.'

'You went out in the monsoon when it was starting to flood?' he asked.

'Someone had to do it. But it was rather frightening.'

'Frightening! I should think so.' The

sympathy in his blue eyes changed to one of surprised admiration.

'How long will it before anyone can use the Ghat road?' I asked.

'I can't say that, I'm afraid. Sometimes they say, quick come, quick go, and the monsoon has been early this time.'

Hanna pattered into the room, and I explained to the doctor that she had been staying with her grandmother when the rains had started, and how Philip thought he would have time to pay two visits to Hush Hush Valley before the monsoon came.

'If it eases off in the next few days, there might be some news,' said Dr Baxter. 'I know the hardest thing to do is sit and wait. I'm pretty busy, but I'll try to call round again. I'll let you know if I hear anything. After the floods have gone, there'll be plenty for me to deal with, no doubt.'

There was a grim, set, look on his face when he said this. Before leaving the house he reminded me that there was absolutely nothing I could do, or that anyone could do until the water subsided a bit. This it did during the next few days, as the wind and rain eased off. The once brown grass was now a vivid emerald green, as Philip had told me it would be. And just when I was wondering if it were possible to see what had happened in Hush Hush Valley, Dr Baxter again called at the house. His face was very grave indeed.

'Mrs Belvedere, have you had word from Hush Hush Valley yet?'

'No,' I said, and sank down into a chair. I began to tremble uncontrollably.

'The road is bad, but passable now. The mail *tonga* got part of the way yesterday, then it broke down. There'll be no *tonga* up the Ghat road tomorrow, but a double bullock-*bandy* should be able to get through. I am prepared to go with you; Mrs Snow has already told me she will accompany you too. And the ayah had better come.'

The room seemed to be spinning

around. 'Dr Baxter, do you know anything?' I managed to ask at last.

'Only that there are many casualties. In any case, a medical man will have to go from here to make a report to the hospital. It may as well be me.'

'What about little Hanna?'

'The ayah had better make arrangements to have her looked after here. We don't want a child with us.'

'And has the monsoon stopped?'

'It will probably rain again in a few days, but I don't think it will reach the same fury.'

After days of wondering what had gone on in Hush Hush Valley, I felt dazed at the prospect of actually going there. At least I will know the worst, I told myself, as the following day, still trembling, I sat in the bullock-*bandy* with a subdued but sympathetic Mrs Snow. When Dr Baxter spoke, it was about the condition of the road, or other strictly practical matters. The ayah crouched in a silent stupor, as the *bandy* got out into the paddy flats beyond the town, jerking and splashing its way along a road which was bad at the best of times.

At the foothills I gave a cry of alarm; it looked like a sea. We would never get through! We went up one incline, and down another; every gully in the laterite road spouted water. That interminable journey up the Ghat road seemed as if it would end in disaster half a dozen times. Again and again we stuck in a welter of mud, but somehow the bullock-cart was pulled out, and we journeyed on with agonizing slowness.

I thought how ironic it was that I had wanted to see Hush Hush Valley so much, and now I was going to see it under these circumstances. As time went by, everyone seemed to be beyond speech. Already it was a murky twilight, although it was still afternoon. Dr Baxter had said there was a rest-house where we could get a meal and stay overnight. I could not believe it; we seemed to have been on this slow, endless trail for a lifetime. Gusts of wind blew into the *bandy*; water spattered and soaked us from the road. It was incomprehensible that Mrs Snow had voluntarily undertaken such a journey. The smell of damp blankets mingled with the smell of beedi, which the driver was smoking.

At last we reached the rest-house. It was a poor sort of place, but because of its strategic position, although reeking with dampness, it was in not too bad a state, considering the severity of the monsoon. The bullocks stood with heaving sides; I felt a pang of pity for the poor, patient beasts. There was a smoky fire inside the rest-house, and a badly trimmed lamp.

But at least we ate a meal of sorts. There were no beds, as such, and we spent the night sleeping fitfully on blankets. In the eerie, grey silence of the following morning, we began to make the descent down into the valley. I gasped with terror more than once, going forward into that muddy slope, when the *bandy* would tilt at a frightening angle.

More terrifying than the wretched journey, though, was the reality when we finally arrived at what had been the village at Hush Hush Valley. The level of the water was dropping now; that coffee-coloured water which had covered those thatched roof bungalows.

The ayah gave a terrible wail, and covered her face with her hands. Mrs Snow put her arm around me, and Dr Baxter said we would have to find out what we could. Something turned cold inside me, and everything took on an unreal quality. It could not be real to see dead, drowned bodies laid out side by side in rows to be identified. It could not be real, I told myself, looking down at the cold, lifeless form of a man. This man was my husband — he was Philip!

'Philip!' I cried. 'Philip!' He could not possibly have lost his life in the floods at Hush Hush Valley, why, he had said he had time to make two journeys there before the rains came. I must be dreaming. It was a long, horrible nightmare that went on and on . . .

Then I heard another cry from the ayah. She was bending down over the body of a girl, a girl with long, black hair.

'Sajoodaye!' she wailed. 'Sajoodaye!'

I felt a strong, comforting arm take hold of mine, and I looked straight into Dr Baxter's blue eyes.

'You have seen enough, Mrs Belvedere,' he said quietly. I saw Mrs Snow trying to comfort the ayah, and nothing seemed a dream any longer. Even through the mind-numbing sense of shock, I knew that this was reality.

My husband and the ayah's daughter had both died in the monsoon at Hush Hush Valley.

14

During the next few weeks the rains stopped and started again, but never with the fury of that first onslaught. People called at the house to see me; everyone was kind and consoling, particularly Mrs Snow. Dr Baxter called frequently, in a capacity half professional, and half as a friend. At first I had needed something to make me sleep at nights; I longed to sleep and forget everything, but that could not go on for ever.

The shock of Philip's death came too soon after the shock of losing the baby. If I had been spared that child, I would have had something to live for. Now everything, meeting Philip, coming to India, my disillusionment and unhappiness, losing the baby, Philip's death — all seemed a kaleidoscope of events, ending in nothing, only sadness and regrets.

'I feel perhaps I could have been more understanding — a better wife to him, somehow,' I said to Mrs Snow.

'Mrs Belvedere, I can't speak ill of the dead, but I won't have you say that. When he brought you to Lebanon as his wife, I felt sympathetic towards you, and I made up my mind I would help you in any way I could. He could have been a much better husband to you.'

I felt a little shock of surprise when she said this.

'I won't say any more,' she went on. 'Naturally, I am sorry about his death. He would have been alive today, if he had stayed in his own home with his wife, though.'

'I know,' I said. 'It was just the way things happened. If only he had waited another day — '

'Try not to dwell on it,' said Mrs Snow. 'Have you made up your mind what you are going to do now?'

'Not really,' I said. 'My aunt and uncle want me to sell up, and go back home.'

'It's for you to decide, my dear.'

After she had gone, I sat thinking about things. And it seemed to me that I'd had enough of India. It had brought me nothing but heartache. I thought of Wiltshire; of rolling hills and green fields, and faces I had known since my childhood. I would go home . . .

There was a shuff-shuff at the door, and the ayah announced Dr Baxter. Since the tragedy of Hush Hush Valley she had been very subdued. Hanna was still with her; I had asked about the child's father, and it seemed he too had died in the floods. Apart from that, I was too involved in my own grief to give much comfort to the ayah. I knew that she was suffering, but she had always been so hostile towards me.

Dr Baxter advanced into the room. 'How are you?' he asked. He was always so kind when he came. I could never forget how wonderful he had been after I had identified Philip's body at Hush Hush Valley. We sat and talked for some time. I told him of Mrs Snow's visit, and how I had decided that my best plan was to go home. He listened thoughtfully.

'You know, when you first came out to India you told me you wanted a challenge from life,' he said. 'Life is offering you a tremendous challenge now, but you are not taking it up.'

I was rather surprised at his attitude. 'I don't really see that,' I said. 'I came here because it was my husband's home; living here was the challenge. But now — well, there is nothing to stay for — ' I broke off, because I was becoming emotional. I said in a voice that was almost inaudible: 'I want to go home.'

'Yes,' he said. 'I can understand that. But if you go home now, you'll be running away. Home; yes, some day, perhaps. But when you go, don't go as a coward, Mrs Belvedere. Not as a coward.'

After he had gone, I sat thinking about his words. Several weeks had passed since Philip's funeral. The sun was beginning to creep back. The flood waters had receded from the factory, although nothing had been done there yet. Early in the monsoon, though, I had arranged with Ernest Jones to pay the coolies during the time they were unable to work. But that was foresight on my part. I had felt that the factory was a stake in the future.

But now — what did it matter? I spent a tossing, uneasy night, during which Dr Baxter's words came back to me again and again: 'Not as a coward . . . not as a coward . . . '

Nevertheless, I intended to write home and tell Aunt Margaret that I was coming to England as soon as I had disposed of the house and property. I put it off for a few days, and then one morning, I took up my pen, and began to write the letter: While I was doing so, the ayah announced a Mr Giuseppe Fattorini.

I looked up in surprise. A middle-aged, smiling Italian advanced, and shook my hand, bowing as he did so. He was thick-set, sleek and prosperous, and very sure of himself.

'Mrs Belvedere, I wish you good day! I have come to offer my condolences on your great loss. So sad — so very sad about your husband — and now you are a young widow — '

'Yes?' I said coldly.

His first effusiveness became slightly subdued. 'Well, shall we say that under the circumstances I have come to make you an offer — one which you would be foolish to refuse.'

'Really?'

He tugged nervously at his black moustache. Hostility rose in me; I knew well enough what his 'offer' would be. I let him continue.

'I mean — well — you are a lady alone now. You cannot handle the tile business, and anyway, they say you will go back to England — sell up. We would wish to be the first to make you an offer for your factory — '

'You have been misinformed,' I said, and even as I spoke, I had a feeling of power, almost of exhilaration. 'I have no intention of selling the factory to anyone, and, I may add, least of all to you, Mr Fattorini. Now I am a very busy person, so I wish you good day.'

His swarthy face flushed; his ingratiating manner dropped from him like a cloak. 'You'll regret this!' he snarled. 'Next time, you will be the one to come to me — and to plead — '

'Plead with you?' I laughed. I could feel my face flushing with anger. 'I would as soon plead with a snake! Now will you kindly be gone?'

In spite of my brave words, I was trembling when he left the house. I looked down at the letter I was writing to Aunt Margaret, and tore it up. Write to her I would, but not to say that I was coming home. Giuseppe Fattorini coming and bidding for the factory like that had changed everything. My fighting spirit, which no longer felt that there was anything worth fighting for, suddenly rose up and revitalized me with new life.

I sent for Ernest Jones, and told him

to get the coolies back into the factory — to get everyone back, with the exception of Bango. I told him that I wanted the place cleaned up, that the *pattimars* could get up the river again now, and that we needed clay, and plenty of it.

'I want you to be my manager,' I told him. 'Together, we will make it the best tile works in the district. The better it is, the more you will benefit.'

For a moment he seemed quite overcome. 'I will do my best, Mrs Belvedere. Thank you,' he managed to say.

'We will have trolley rails put down, and anything else you think is a good idea,' I said. 'I don't know much about tile making yet, but I will learn.'

'We need the best workmen and the best clay,' he said simply. 'Perhaps later, new kilns, and even a steam plant, instead of bullocks . . . but that is looking ahead.'

'We'll get them,' I assured him. The house was mine; the factory was mine, and I had some money, if not as much as formerly. Ahead of me lay hard work and struggle, but I was determined to succeed.

And now, with the sweet, almost second spring of a Sadura autumn upon us, there was no unbearable heat to sap my energy. I toiled late and early at the factory. Every morning I was there, going through the accounts with Ernest, getting to know the workers, finding out the quickest and easiest way to do things. It was a source of great satisfaction to me when once again we were manufacturing tiles.

I saw the river clay being brought in, being dumped in the jetty sheds, and going through the mills, before being carried in wet slices to the presses. I saw the mould being slid into the press, the press come down, and the tiles going along a sort of shute to where a couple of boys oiled them with kerosene and coconut oil. Every tile was marked with a cedar tree on the back — proof that they had come from the Lebanon tile works. Soon the drying lofts were full of tiles. Every day I learned something more. By night time I was tired, too tired for much social life.

My activities at the factory met with a mixed reception from my circle of friends and acquaintances at Sadura.

'It's no place for a woman, surely?' was the reaction from the Radstocks.

'It's very unfeminine, going into the factory like that. Don't you think so?' from Rosalie Dysart.

'I haven't really thought about that,' I said. 'What would you do in my position?' I added, with just a trace of tartness.

'Me? Oh, I would go home, I suppose.'

'I could go home any time. But I've chosen to stay, and try and make a success of the tile works.'

'And good luck to you,' said Mr Snow heartily. 'Emily and I think Mrs Belvedere is to be admired. It takes courage to stay in a place where you have suffered grievous losses — and most of us haven't got that kind of courage.'

I could tell that remark did not please Miss Dysart. She cast a quick glance in the direction of Dr Baxter, obviously hoping that he had not heard it. To her chagrin, he had.

'I quite agree,' he said quietly. 'I always try to encourage grieving people to fill their lives with activity. So many merely sit and feel sorry for themselves.'

We were spending an evening at the Snows. I was becoming accustomed to going about by myself now. That evening, though, Dr Baxter, who had walked to the Snows, offered to accompany me back in the bullock-coach.

'I hear that Fattorinis, the Italian tile-makers, are hoping to edge you out of business altogether,' he said.

'Yes, I know. Fattorini tried to get me to sell the factory to them. It was that which made me decide to stay, and make a success of it. I've made Ernest Jones manager, and I know he is trustworthy. I got rid of Bango, that awful foreman who drank. But I really need a good foreman — it's too much for Ernest, running between the office and the factory all day.'

'M'mm, it's a problem. I agree. Perhaps you and Ernest could look for the best, most trustworthy worker, and see about making him foreman.'

For a while we sat talking in the bullock-coach. Then Dr Baxter helped me down, and said that he would walk home. I entered the silent house; the loneliness seemed to press down on me.

If only Philip had cared more about the business — if only he had employed a good foreman in the first place. I sat in the bedroom, brushing my hair, seeing my engagement ring sparkle in the lamplight; that ring which had been paid for by my own money. I had closed the door of Philip's dressing room, with everything in as he had left it. Somehow his personality lingered on.

He had been so different from Dr Baxter, I thought. I wondered how things were between the doctor and Miss Dysart. As she had once remarked to me, he seemed devoted to his work. As I thought of her, I thought of that girl who had taken her life because her parents had disapproved of Philip. Miss Dysart would never do that for any man, I reflected, as I climbed into bed.

She's calculating; Dr Baxter is too good for her, I thought, with a little shock of surprise. Then I fell to thinking about my own problems. Out of common humanity I had allowed the ayah to continue in her duties about the house, but I did not care for the idea as a permanent arrangement. Then there was the coffee-garden over at Hush Hush Valley. I knew that I would have to go there, now that the floods were over. And this time I would go alone. I thought about the planter friend whom Philip had stayed with. Had he survived the floods? I must find out.

When I told the ayah I was going to Hush Hush Valley, she asked very quietly if she might accompany me, and bring Hanna, too. For a moment I hesitated. Then I thought that she knew the place after all; there would be no language difficulty with her there; she would be very useful. Probably she had reasons for wanting to go there, too.

Certainly I was determined not to ask any of the Sadura ladies to accompany me. I could never forget Mrs Snow travelling with me on that nightmare journey during the rains. She had done more than enough.

I told Babwah to look after the house, and gave instructions to Ernest Jones concerning the factory. And early one morning we left the house, and took the long trail up the Ghat road, in a *tonga* this time. It was not a happy journey by any means, although conditions were much pleasanter than they had been the first time. The ayah was very quiet. She was different in the house these days; she no longer listened at doors, no longer seemed to be watching me. She carried out her tasks mechanically, and looked after Hanna. The child, too, was quiet on the journey, except when she occasionally chattered to her grandmother. Everywhere was fresh and lovely after the rains; it was as though the whole countryside had been reborn.

The following day, after staying at the rest-house again, I had to brace myself for my first sight of Hush Hush Valley since the monsoon. It looked very different now. It was green and blooming; out of the chaos of mud and disaster, people had picked up the threads of their lives again. Huts were being rebuilt, repairs attended to. It was amazing that a place could look so different in so short a time.

I had asked the ayah if she knew where a Mr Cyril Hauser lived, but she said she had never heard of him. I had hoped to visit him, and try to find out something about Philip's last hours — that was if Mr Hauser had been spared. But all enquiries about him proved futile.

I felt completely baffled.

'I want to see Sajoodaye's place,' said the ayah.

'I'll have to see the coffee-garden,' I said. 'I'll have to decide what to do with it.'

'Ye-es. This is the way to the coffee-garden.'

'But you want to see your daughter's place.'

'Ye-es. She was in coffee-garden.'

For a moment I was too taken aback to say a word. So the ayah's daughter had actually lived on the coffee estate — and I had not known until now! Oh, Philip . . . the old heartbreak and sadness at his constant deceitfulness came back. There was no Cyril Hauser in the district, and never had been. And why hadn't he told me that the ayah's daughter had a bungalow in the coffee-garden? Why should I mind; I'd had to accept the idea that the ayah and her family were treated with special consideration by him. In silence we walked together to Sajoodaye's bungalow.

A native called Singh lived not far away, and worked on the coffee plantation. He had managed to survive the floods, and he told us all about it, half in Telugu, half in English. Sajoo-daye's bungalow had been completely covered by the water, apparently. People had taken to the roofs when they had been unexpectedly trapped by the swirling water; he gesticulated, and pointed to the roof of the house. The bungalow had been ransacked, which was hardly surprising. The rooms were bare, and full of dried mud. On the floor was a mud-caked, plaster saint, and there were a few boxes and odds and ends left lying about.

The ayah began to argue with Singh; he shrugged, and indicated that it was nothing to do with him. I walked outside and let them fight it out. What did it matter, anyway? But as I stood there, a thought came to me which seemed to be the ideal solution to the problem of the ayah.

Why couldn't she take over Sajoo-daye's bungalow? Indeed, why couldn't she oversee the running of the coffee plantation? I knew that she was shrewd, and not easily taken in by her own kind. Trustworthy? Well, probably as trustworthy as anyone else I would get. I wanted her out of Lebanon, but as humanely as possible. There was poor little Hanna to think of, too. The floods had orphaned her. I walked back into the bungalow.

'Do you know anything about coffee, Ayah? About growing it, I mean?' I asked.

She looked slightly taken aback. 'A bi-it,' she replied cautiously. 'I have seen it grown. Ye-es, I know a bit.'

I indicated to Singh that he could go, and he went outside, still protesting that he'd had nothing to do with the ransacking of the bungalow. I turned to the ayah.

'Would you like to come here with Hanna? You could bring all your stuff, and take care of the coffee-garden here. If you do well, I will pay you well. Otherwise, I will sell it.'

For a moment she looked quite stricken.

'I am sorry you can find nothing that belonged to your daughter,' I went on. 'I am sorry about all your troubles, but I cannot have you and Hanna at Lebanon for ever. My husband would not have wanted you to suffer hardship, though. Will you come here?'

After some hesitation, she spoke. 'Very well. If you wish it, I will come.'

There was something utterly resigned about her voice. It was as though she no longer cared, now. I hurried outside, and called back the native. He came towards me hopefully.

'You knew Mr Belvedere, the *dorai*?' I asked.

'Ye-es, memsahib.'

'I am Mrs Belvedere. Do you know where he was at the time of the floods?'

'I don' know — no. Everyone was afraid, running away.'

'Did you see him at all?'

'I saw him go to the bungalow . . . I never saw him after that.'

'When did you see him at the bungalow?' A shrug was the only reply.

I gave up the idea of finding anything out from Singh.

'Will you clean up the house?' I asked him. 'Clean it up, do what you can — and do what you can with the coffee plantation, too. It isn't very big . . . you are lucky, you have been saved from the floods.' I rattled the rupees in my purse.

'I will be back. You will be well paid,' I went on.

'Yes, yes, all will be done, memsahib,' he said eagerly. I counted out some money. The ayah had come to the door, and was watching me.

'The house will be made ready for you,' I said. She nodded, and by mutual consent we left the bungalow, with Hanna running and skipping in front of us.

No doubt the ayah had told her some story; certainly not that her parents had gone for good; in any case, so young a child could not understand death. She had been very quiet in the bungalow, as if frightened by something she could not explain. Now she seemed glad that we were leaving. Well, she would soon be coming back to Hush Hush Valley for good, I thought.

On the journey back, I considered my future plans. I would have to visit Hush Hush Valley again, and I really needed Ernest Jones with me, to help sort things out, and get the place on a reasonable business footing. There was much to be done.

Hanna had fallen asleep, and the ayah was deep in thought, staring ahead. Perhaps she was pleased to be leaving Lebanon; well pleased to go. I was certainly well pleased at the prospect of being without her.

15

My plans concerning the ayah proceeded smoothly. As soon as possible she was installed at Hush Hush Valley, and I felt as if a great weight had been lifted from me. And on Ernest Jones' recommendation, I engaged the services of Zillah, a charming Eurasian girl. She was an excellent needlewoman, and helpful in every way. She was more than that; she was a companion to me, as well as a maid. She had been taught by the nuns at the Convent of The Sacred Heart in Sadura, and she was quite well read.

I installed her in Philip's dressing room, not without a little pang. Often, before retiring, we would have long talks together, while she was brushing my hair. I knew that whatever we discussed was just between the two of us; she was not a gossip.

About this time the tile factory had two strokes of good luck. The first was that one of our agents knew where there was a second-hand steam engine for sale, very cheap. We bought it immediately. Ernest said we could have trolleys, machine presses and pug-mills all worked by it. When I mentioned it to Mr Snow, to my surprise and gratitude, he offered to overhaul the engine, and take charge of having it installed. Naturally we couldn't do everything at once, but we got the pug-mills going, and said goodbye to the bullocks. We were making progress.

But more than that, I no longer lay awake at night thinking of Philip, or grieving for what might have been. For one thing, I was too tired physically, and for another, I had so many other things to think of.

I still saw a good deal of the Snows; indeed, I considered them my best friends in Sadura, among the married couples. Mrs Snow mothered me, while her husband kept a watchful eye on other things. I still saw Dr Baxter occasionally, too, but he no longer called at the house in a half friendly, half professional capacity.

'I'm glad you are managing to cope with the factory so well. I'm glad, too that the ayah has gone, and that you now have a suitable companion,' he said. It was while he was playing in a cricket match, and I was watching, just as I had done when Philip was alive.

'Thank you — I'm managing very well,' I said.

'You have little social life these days, though. I suppose this is partly because you are in mourning, and partly because you are too busy. Mrs Snow said she had to persuade you to come here.'

'You seem to be increasingly busy yourself,' I reminded him.

'Yes, there is more and more work to do. Ever since the monsoon we have had cases of cholera coming into the hospital, mostly from up the river. If there is a real epidemic — ' he broke off, his face grave.

'Do you think there might be an epidemic?' I asked.

'I hope not. But I don't discount the possibility.' He went in to bat, and I exchanged chit-chat with the other ladies. Rosalie Dysart was there, her eyes frequently turning in the direction of David Baxter. I thought of how she had once told me the qualities she would look for in a husband. Undoubtedly she thought she had found them in him.

I remembered meeting him that day when I had been to the factory. How kind he had been. He had taken me for a drive, and I had talked to him about my problems. Well, those particular problems had gone, I thought sadly. I no longer had a husband to cause me worry; I no longer heard the shuff-shuff of the ayah's feet. I was a widow now, with a fresh set of problems to cope with.

I left the cricket match some time later feeling lonely and depressed. This mood lasted until the next day, when a large and rather imposing looking Indian appeared in the office. He said his name was Chilwa Ragoobir, and that he had worked for Giuseppe Fattorini as his foreman at the tile works. It seemed, though, that Fattorini had thought he could make free with Ragoobir's young daughter; that the man was in no position to protest.

'I te-ell him I no-ot stand for his dirty ways,' he explained in his halting, sing-song English. 'So he tell me to go.'

'Yes?' I said. Ernest Jones and I exchanged glances.

'They say you wa-anting one foreman here. Is so?'

Ernest cleared his throat, and looked at me.

'That is correct,' I said slowly. How good was he as a foreman? Was his story true? Was he trustworthy? Or was he just sent to spy on us? We could soon find out.

'I would wo-ork hard for you, memsahib.'

'I would like to have you, if things are as you say,' I said cautiously.

'My wife and daughter wait outside.'

'Bring them in then,' I told him.

He produced them; a dignified and handsome woman, and an incredibly beautiful girl, with a skin so fair it was no more than olive.

'Tell the memsahib about Mr Fattorini,' he said to his daughter. She immediately burst into tears and hid her face. There seemed to be an air of authenticity about the story.

'Shall I make further enquiries?' asked Ernest.

I hesitated. Once I would have taken the man on trust, and believed him. Marriage to Philip had made me wary, though.

'It might be as well,' I said. I explained to the man that we must find out from other sources if his story was true. If it was, we would be pleased to employ him. I told him to come back in a few days' time, and to show my goodwill, I gave him a few rupees. He went away looking considerably more cheerful.

To our great relief, the man's story was true, and so Chilwa Ragoobir came to work for us, and I never regretted it for a moment. He knew all there was to know about tiles; he knew how to haggle with the boatmen over the price of clay; he knew where to send the agents for fresh business. And above all, he was sober and good living. That was our second stroke of good luck. Now, at last, although I still visited the factory every day, it meant that I had a bit more leisure.

My satisfaction was short-lived. Two of the sorters complained of feeling unwell, and Ragoobir sent them home. He looked grave. 'The cholera — it is coming, memsahib,' he said fearfully. I looked at Ernest.

'It is true,' he said. 'At first it was up-river, but now it is coming to Sadura. Already the hospital is full.'

I went home feeling very worried, to find scant comfort there. An aunt of

Zillah's had been stricken, and was gravely ill.

'They have not enough doctors nor enough nurses in that hospital,' she said. I could see that she had been crying, and suddenly I felt the fear that was running through Sadura. I had seen nothing of Dr Baxter recently; I had seen nothing of the Snows, either, for about a fortnight. I ordered the bullock-coach, and drove round to their bungalow. Mr Snow was in alone, and he was not his usual, cheerful self.

'Ah, Mrs Belvedere! I am sorry my wife is not here. She is helping at the hospital.'

'Helping at the hospital?' I repeated.

'Yes. The cholera epidemic is growing rapidly, and they are short of nurses. Not that I approve of Emily going nursing at her age — I think she's done enough. But she says as long as she is needed, she will go. How are things with you, my dear?'

'Quite satisfactory just now. The steam engine is going well, and as you have heard, we now have a good foreman. But two of our sorters had to go home ill — ' I broke off. What I was saying sounded so self-centred, in view of the fact that the town was facing an onslaught of cholera. And Mrs Snow had gone to help up at that primitive looking hospital! I began to feel rather ashamed of myself. 'I didn't know — I didn't realize things were so bad,' I explained. 'I've been so wrapped up in the factory lately.'

'Well, that's understandable. But they are desperately in need of volunteers to help.'

'I see,' I said slowly. 'Well, now I know, perhaps I can do something.'

'It is not pleasant,' said Mr Snow, quietly. 'Put romantic notions of nursing to one side if you go to that place. It is depressing and terrible, and there is the risk of infection.'

I noticed, though, he had not said 'Don't go'. And, indeed, why should he, with his own wife, a much older woman, uncomplainingly going there every day? That evening I talked things over with Zillah. She agreed that she would accompany me to the hospital the next day, and volunteer to help, although she admitted that she was afraid. So was I, and yet it seemed that to stand to one side at a time like this was an act of gross selfishness.

Sadura hospital was brick built, with wooden verandahs; a poor looking place, but within these walls men and women were battling desperately to save the lives of others. The smell of disinfectant mingled with other smells, making me feel slightly faint. I asked the Eurasian nurse in charge if I might speak to Dr Baxter.

'Dr Baxter is ve-ery busy — ' she began.

'Please say it is Mrs Belvedere. I am anxious to see him,' I said briskly. After a moment's hesitation, she disappeared through the door which led to the wards. Zillah and I sat without speaking. After what seemed a long time, Dr Baxter stood in front of us. He looked tired and worn, and far from pleased at seeing me.

'Mrs Belvedere, what are you doing here?' was his brusque greeting. I was rather taken aback.

'I — well, I heard you were in need of nursing volunteers,' I stammered. 'I haven't had any experience, but I'm sure I could help — ' I broke off; he looked so angry.

'You have no right to come here like this. You should have enough sense to keep away. You are at risk — don't you understand?'

'I understand perfectly,' I said, nettled by his annoyance. 'I have come to offer my services, the same as Mrs Snow — and other women who live in Sadura, I've no doubt.' I think my spirited retort surprised him. He lifted up his hand, and smoothed his hair in a sudden gesture of weariness.

'I can't ask this of you,' he said. 'It is terrible here — and likely to get worse. I don't want you here. You are too — ' He broke off.

301

'We want to help,' I said calmly. 'Zillah and I both want to.'

'No. I forbid it,' he said.

'You can't. Nobody can forbid me to do anything.' It was true, I was my own mistress.

'Well, if you are determined to come, then come you must,' he agreed, his face grim. 'But against my better judgement, Mrs Belvedere. And you must follow instructions — you must take every precaution to protect yourself.'

'I will,' I promised. He was not pleased, but I knew that I had won. So Zillah and I became volunteer nurses at the dreaded Sadura hospital. I had not known up to then how devastating an epidemic could be. The staff were hard pressed, and I seemed clumsy and stupid in my first attempts at nursing. To be surrounded day after day by the sick and dying was something I felt I could never get used to. Mr Snow had been right when he had said there was nothing romantic about it. Not only was it hard work, but a great deal of it was extremely distasteful.

Fortunately it was one of the best times of the year as far as the climate was concerned. I did not think I could possibly have coped during the hot weather. Zillah and I fell into a routine. Every morning I visited the factory while she attended to the household affairs. After tiffin we had a brief rest, and then the bullock-coach would take us to the hospital. Lebanon reeked of disinfectant; Zillah and I did everything Mrs Snow told us we must do to avoid falling victims of the disease.

'I've nursed through cholera before,' she told us. 'Some day they will get a vaccine against it, I'm convinced. Not yet, though. But you two are young and strong and willing — and that's more than some people are. Young and strong, perhaps, but not willing.'

Day followed day, and each night Zillah and I went home exhausted. Dr Baxter was always there after we had gone. I had not sought him out after my first visit to the hospital, when he had shown his disapproval so clearly. Now that I was actually there, though, he often had a brief word with me.

'Are you sure you are not doing too much? You are still attending to factory matters, I understand,' he said one day.

'We are managing very well,' I assured him. 'I am getting more used to it now — I mean, I'm getting a bit better at nursing. The staff here are very nice to us volunteers.'

'I should think so,' he said shortly, but before he could say any more, he was called away to see a patient.

He had changed, I thought, a little sadly. His attitude was polite, but he didn't want me there. Of course, he was rushed off his feet; worked to death; I could hardly expect him to make charming conversation in that place.

My life at Sadura had shrunk to alternating between the factory, the hospital, and home. The output at the tile works had dropped considerably owing to the epidemic, but the same thing was happening everywhere.

'Miss Dysart and her parents have left the district for a while,' said Mrs Snow one day. 'Like a lot more, they've gone to Ootocamund until the cholera epidemic is over. Well, they'll be safe enough there.'

'I thought Miss Dysart might have volunteered to help,' I said. We were at the bedside of a young boy. How merciless and disgusting this disease was, I thought. It was running its course cruelly and fatally with this youthful victim. 'I have seen nothing of her lately,' I added.

Mrs Snow gave a short, derisive laugh. 'Who has? No one who comes to this hospital.'

I looked up sharply. 'No one?' I began, then checked myself.

'Indeed, no. We are little better than lepers to Miss Dysart.'

'I thought — I mean, from what she once said to me, I gathered that she admired people who — well, who did these sort of things,' I finished, rather lamely.

'In theory, no doubt!'

'Men who did their duty — who had an aim in life,' I went on, almost to myself.

'As long as that aim in life does not inconvenience Miss Dysart. She will find more entertainment in the Hills, I have no doubt.'

Mrs Snow's words lingered in my mind. Was that why Dr Baxter seemed so brusque? Had he and Miss Dysart quarrelled because he was giving so much of his attention to the hospital? Or had he not wanted her in Sadura at all? Had he persuaded her to go to the Hills for safety? It seemed more than likely. But somehow, I wanted him to talk to me in the old, friendly way again. Perhaps, though, he thought that I was now over the worst of my grief after Philip's death, and that I could fend for myself. I supposed in a way this was true enough.

Every night I tumbled into bed, and slept heavily out of sheer exhaustion. The days when Philip had been alive seemed quite dreamlike now; I had no time to brood. I had no time for anything very much, beyond the factory and the hospital. I still wrote letters home, but did not mention that Sadura was in the grip of cholera. I only hoped that the epidemic would not get so bad that reports of it appeared in the English newspapers.

Zillah was leading just as exhausting a life as I was, but she never complained. It was her own decision to nurse at the hospital; I had never tried to persuade her. A steady stream of patients were still coming in; one day an old man was brought in, apparently in the last stages of the illness.

'It's Chitteranjan, the devil-dancer,' said Mrs Snow. 'You remember him, don't you?'

'Yes,' I said. 'I remember him.' I tried to fight down the distaste I felt. I thought of that evening when we had all gone up on the ridge, and he had prophesied death to so many people there.

He had ranted of floods and sickness, and he had been right; he had told Philip he would die, and he had been right. Had he known his own future, too? I shuddered. He suddenly opened his sunken eyes and looked at me. He muttered something, but it was not in English.

'What is he saying?' I asked Mrs Snow. She shook her head, uncomprehending. The devil-dancer seemed to stop in mid-sentence. He gave a kind of choking cough, and I felt as if I had had as much as I could stand just then. I walked away from the bedside, and almost bumped into Dr Baxter.

'Mrs Belvedere — are you all right? What — ' he broke off, and looked across at the bed I had just left.

'It's the devil-dancer,' I said abruptly. 'I think he's — '

Dr Baxter pushed past me on his way to the bedside. I hurried out of that wretched ward, and stood for a while on the corridor. Not that it was quiet there; it was not quiet anywhere at that place. Even at the entrance, weeping relatives of patients gathered at all hours of the day. I was convinced that the old man had recognized me, and that he had tried to tell me something. But I didn't wish to hear it. I plunged my hands into disinfectant; my hands, would they ever be soft and smooth again, when all this was over? Later, I heard that Chitteranjan had died, and that the ayah had come to Sadura to do what was necessary. I thought no more about it until one day a woman and child were admitted to the hospital together.

'It's the ayah and Hanna,' said Mrs Snow, her voice disbelieving. 'Poor little Hanna . . . '

I gave an involuntary cry as I saw the stick-like limbs and still form of what had once been a healthy child.

'We might pull her through,' said Dr Baxter, who had come unnoticed beside me. 'She seems to have it in the milder form — and more and more are getting the milder form now. But not the ayah, I'm afraid.'

16

It had been a shock to see both the ayah and Hanna come into the hospital. I felt not only pity, but something resembling remorse. If I had kept them at Lebanon, perhaps they would not have fallen victims of the epidemic. I mentioned this to Zillah.

'You cannot know these things,' she said. 'They may have caught it in any case. Nobody can foresee these happenings.'

Mrs Snow said much the same. 'You did not treat her badly — you set her up in Hush Hush Valley, which was more than a lot of women in your position would have done. She may not have caught it there, anyway. She could just as well become infected when she came back to Sadura, to attend to her brother's affairs.'

I saw the ayah differently now. She

was no longer an enemy; just a pitifully sick woman, helpless and striken, like the other patients. Little Hanna was infinitely more pitiful. The three of us, Zillah, Mrs Snow, and myself felt that whatever happened, we must save Hanna. I felt that Dr Baxter was moved by the same spirit, and yet, he did not neglect his duties towards any other patient.

There was a special sadness about all the children who fell victims to the disease, but I had known Hanna, had listened to her funny little giggle, and had felt her hand clasped trustingly in mine. In the crowded ward where the children lay, I was at Hanna's bedside whenever possible. I had sat with other children who were dying, but the thought of that happening to her was quite unbearable.

I willed her to get better. I stopped going to the factory at all, now, and spent every available minute at the hospital.

One of the volunteer nurses, a white

woman, had succumbed to the disease herself, and died. It made me realize afresh the danger we were all in at that place.

'You are spending too much time here, Mrs Belvedere,' said Dr Baxter grimly, one day. 'After all, you are a volunteer, not a member of the nursing staff — ' He broke off, and shook his head.

I was exhausted, and it must have shown on my face. 'It's Hanna,' I explained. 'I suppose it's because I know her — '

He gave me a long, searching glance. 'The child is holding her own,' he said. 'Go back home and rest. I insist upon it.'

'You can't insist — ' I began. I could feel myself flushing.

'I'm supposed to be your doctor,' he said curtly. 'Go home, and take Zillah with you. Rest, and don't come back until tomorow afternoon, and not then, if you don't feel better.'

'What about Mrs Snow?' I asked.

'Mrs Snow has plenty of stamina. Besides, she's nursed before many a time; she doesn't get too involved with the patients. I assure you, everything will be done to save Hanna — and the ayah, if it's possible. Now just be sensible, and go home.'

Reluctantly I told Zillah what he had said, and we left the hospital together. Zillah, although very slight in build, was stronger than might have been thought. I think she was alarmed at my obvious fatigue, and she begged me to lie down and rest, once we were back in the house. The following morning I stayed late in bed, and felt much revived.

Zillah and I reported back to the hospital, to find that Hanna was much better.

Not so the ayah. Looking down at her pinched face, I knew that the end was near. Dr Baxter told me as much when he saw me in the ward.

'But Hanna will pull through,' he added. He left Mrs Snow and me at the ayah's bedside. The dark eyes in the wasted face stared straight ahead.

'You know me, Ayah?' I asked. I had not expected any response, but to my surprise the eyes lost their dimness for a moment, and focussed on me.

'Hanna?' she whispered hoarsely.

'She is better,' I said. 'Better.'

It was strange to think now how I had disliked her, and how unhappy her presence in the house had made me. I felt great pity for her at that moment.

'Ta-ake care of her,' came the hoarse whisper. 'You must ta-ake care of her. She is your husband's child.'

Transfixed with surprise, I stared at her. Mrs Snow put out a reassuring hand and rested it lightly on my arm, as if to protect me.

'What — what on earth do you mean?' I managed to stammer. A sense of shock ran right through me.

'Sajoodaye . . . Mr Philip . . . long time together . . . he move her to Hush Hush Valley when Hanna coming . . . he ha-ad a right to marry her . . . '

She stopped speaking; the effort was

too much. I began to tremble. Even though I wanted to cry out that it was not true, something inside me told me that it was true. But it couldn't be true — it couldn't! I turned to Mrs Snow.

'Do you hear what she is saying?' I began, but stopped abruptly. I could see compassion in her eyes, and more than that. Knowledge.

'It's not true!' I cried. She slipped a comforting arm around me.

'Say it isn't true,' I begged.

'My dear, I'm afraid it is true, if she says so. One hears these rumours — '

The ayah's lips quivered; two tears gathered, and ran slowly down her face. 'Ta-ake Hanna,' she urged again, her voice breaking. 'Mr Philip loved her, even though he not ma-ake Sajoodaye his wife. Now both dead — '

Looking down at her, I felt as if I were living through a dream. The child, Hanna — Philip's and Sajoodaye's! A host of little jigsaw pieces seemed to be fitting themselves together, even as I stood there, willing it not to be true.

Mrs Snow took the ayah's pulse.

'She won't speak again,' she said. 'But out of compassion, tell her you'll take Hanna.'

'Why should I?' I asked bitterly. 'I know now why she never wanted me at Lebanon — and she lost my baby for me. I know that too.'

Contrary to Mrs Snow's statement, the ayah did speak again. She had heard what I had said.

'No, I di-id not lose you the baby,' came her whisper. 'I to-old the doctor what I gave you. I told him true.'

'She will be telling the truth,' said Mrs Snow. 'She will not die with that on her conscience.'

'But you never wanted me in the house,' I said.

'No. I wa-anted him to marry Sajoodaye. Ta-ake Hanna . . . ta-ake Hanna . . . '

Her voice was like a sigh, now. I knelt by the bed. 'Very well, I'll take Hanna,' I said.

The next moment I turned on my

heel, and left the ward. Blindly, scarcely knowing what I was doing, I walked into the children's ward. I went over to Hanna's bed, and stood looking at her. She was asleep. Her black hair was neatly plaited, and her long eyelashes lay like dark crescents on her white cheeks. She was going to recover; there was no doubt about that now.

'Yes, she is doing well,' came a voice at my elbow. It was Dr Baxter, and to my surprise and dismay, I burst into tears.

'What is wrong?' he asked, and I heard the old note of kindness in his voice.

'I can't tell you here,' I managed to say. I added that the ayah was dying.

'But that is not the cause of your grief,' he said, and it was a statement, not a question.

I shook my head. 'It's — I can't tell you,' I said. 'I've had the most terrible shock. I — ' It was impossible to go on.

'Don't try to tell me now.' His voice was very quiet. 'Later on — this evening

— I will call at your house and see you. It can't be as bad as all that.'

'It is!' I said vehemently. 'You don't understand.'

'I will when you tell me. I'm going to see the ayah now. Cheer up, the epidemic is on the wane; far fewer cases reported, and a milder from of cholera when they are.'

He gave me an encouraging smile, and left me. I was still stunned with the ayah's revelation. I felt I could discuss it with no one just then. I had no doubt Mrs Snow knew things; had known them all along, and remained silent. But the child, Hanna — what of her? I had promised to take her, urged on by Mrs Snow. An act of forgiveness and compassion on my part . . . but why should I be bound by a promise made like that? And how could Philip have done what he did? Kept that girl at Hush Hush Valley with her child, and visited them whenever possible, and all the time he had been married to me. It was cruel — cruel. I felt I had endured enough before, but this final revelation of the ayah's was the ultimate humiliation.

The memory of that letter I had found flashed into my mind. Now I knew what that girl had meant by 'certain practices' which were tolerated out in India. With a tremendous effort I tried to pull myself together, telling myself that I would soon be going home. I left the children's ward with a last glance at Hanna. When I walked, my legs felt quite weak.

That day, the ayah died. I did not mention what she had told me to Zillah, as we went home together. Instead, I tried to act as if everything was normal, telling her quite cheerfully that the epidemic was on the wane. After dinner, though, I told her the doctor was calling to see me, and she discreetly left me alone in the drawing room. When he entered the room, I thought how tired and drawn he looked, and how the strain of the past few weeks had told on him.

I poured him out a glass of brandy, and, although I rarely had anything beyond a glass of wine, I kept him company with a brandy myself.

'Now,' he said, 'tell me what you are so upset about. Is it connected with the ayah?'

I nodded, and gulped down some brandy. 'She wants me to take her grandchild, Hanna,' I managed to say at last.

'I see,' he said thoughtfully.

'She wanted me to promise,' I said. 'Mrs Snow urged me to, and because the ayah was dying, I did. But the woman caused me nothing but trouble when she was at Lebanon, and now I've promised to take the child. I don't know what to do.'

'Is that all?' he asked, setting down his glass.

'No . . . she says that Hanna is — ' I paused. It couldn't be true — it couldn't!

'That Hanna is — what?'

'Philip's child,' I managed to say,

although my voice sounded strange and far away. 'His — and her daughter's.' Suddenly all my self-control crumpled. I began to sob hopelessly.

'Don't distress yourself so — please! It is a great shock for you, I know — '

'You knew!' I cried, between sobs. 'You knew! Everyone knew! Everyone except me — '

For a moment he said nothing, while I wept. When he did speak, his voice was very gentle. 'There were rumours, yes. There were a number of unsavoury rumours about your late husband. Then he went to England, and returned with you as his bride. What could people do? You were married to him, and anyway, it was nobody else's business — '

'Why did he marry me?' I cried. 'Why?'

He did not speak.

'You know more, don't you? There are still things which I don't know — '

'Mrs Belvedere, I feel I cannot repeat things like that to you. You must ask Mrs Snow. She knew Philip's mother

321

long ago; I believe she was fond of her, and helped her — '

'Helped her?' I said. 'In what way?' I had stopped crying. Something inside me refused to be shocked any more.

'I understand she drank very heavily.'

Suddenly I felt that the last few scales sticking to my eyes concerning Philip had fallen away. 'His whole background was disreputable,' I said. 'That is what you are trying to tell me, isn't it?'

'Something like that — yes. I was his doctor; I cannot comment freely on these things. I am your doctor, too, remember.'

'Yes,' I said, a little bitterly. 'You are very professional these days.' To my surprise, I saw a hurt look in his blue eyes, but somehow, at that moment, I wanted to hurt him.

'How can I be otherwise?' he asked, and there was nothing I could say to that.

'There was a girl who took her own life,' I went on. 'Dorothy Forrester. Did you know her?'

'Yes. They sent for me — '

'They sent for you when they found her dead,' I said slowly. 'That is what you were going to say. Why did she take her own life?'

'I cannot tell you that, Mrs Belvedere. She poisoned herself; it was a very tragic case.'

'Yes, you can tell me. It was something to do with Philip, wasn't it? I have a letter she wrote; I found it in a book one day. I didn't destroy it, I just put it back.'

I went upstairs, and returned with it. Without speaking I handed it to him; that pathetic letter penned by a girl passionately in love. In silence he read it, and handed it back.

'Dorothy Forrester was madly in love with him, I believe,' he said at last. 'Her parents did not approve, for various reasons.'

'His drinking, his gambling, his Indian girl with her child,' I said. 'Why try to shield me from these things? Was there talk of marriage between those two?'

'She hadn't long joined her parents from England. She was their only child, and they were quite wealthy people. They raised objections.'

'And drove her to her death,' I said. 'Otherwise, I suppose he would have married her.'

'I suppose he would. But he left Sadura and went to England until the gossip died down a bit. And there, he met you.'

'Yes,' I said sadly. 'And how naïve, how trusting I was in those days! I fell in love with him at first sight; I thought it was exactly the same with him. I used to feel impatient with my aunt and uncle, the way they talked about knowing nothing about him, and all the rest of it.'

'Well, we all have to face bitter things in our lives, I'm afraid.'

'I've faced a lot during the past twelve months. I believe Philip had been told there was money to come to me. Oddly enough, I didn't know until my uncle and the solicitor told me.

Philip pretended to be very surprised.'

'Mrs Belvedere, I know how painful all this must be to you. Your husband was very attractive to women, and he knew it. He did not care about his business concerns as he should have done; he spent money foolishly, and I believe he wanted a wife with money, but young and attractive, too. Miss Forrester was a likely candidate, but her parents were opposed to him, and not without cause.'

I thought of our reconciliation, after I had recovered from the loss of the baby. I had thought that things were going to be better between us. Now I knew beyond all doubt that things would never have been better. Philip had gone back to Hush Hush Valley to see that girl. There would always have been Sajoodaye — and the ayah. And now there was Hanna.

'But the child — Hanna. Mrs Snow urged me to promise to take her, to give the ayah peace of mind,' I said. 'I feel I am bound by a promise I did not willingly give. The ayah never wanted me in that house; she wanted Philip to marry Sajoodaye.'

'The ayah was a scheming woman, I grant you. She had a hold over your husband, and she knew it. But of course, he would never have married Sajoodaye; she knew that, too. He would never have dismissed the ayah, though.'

'She denied in the hospital that she had given me anything to make me lose the child, and Mrs Snow said she would be telling the truth. I know she was glad I had lost the baby, though.'

'Undoubtedly. A child of yours might have loosened the hold Sajoodaye had on account of Hanna.'

'Yes; Hanna,' I said slowly. 'What will become of her, if I don't take her?'

'That I cannot tell you. I know the ayah wasn't a Christian, but Sajoodaye may well have been converted. You must ask Mrs Snow. If there is nobody else to take her, in that case, I've no doubt the good sisters at the Sacred

Heart Convent will take her.'

I sat thinking this over. Somehow I felt that I wanted Dr Baxter to say more; to tell me the best thing to do.

'It would be a tremendous task to take that child and bring her up,' I said, half to myself.

'A tremendous task. An act of great charity, and great courage, too. Not to mention forgiveness.'

Forgiveness — yes. To adopt Hanna and bring her up, knowing that she was my husband's love child by Sajoodaye . . . How could anyone be expected to do such a thing?

'You must think about it, Mrs Belvedere. Meanwhile, I want you to promise to rest tomorrow. I've told Mrs Snow she's done enough at that hospital, too. The worst is over; you have done very well, and Zillah too. You have the factory to attend to, and quite a number of problems, so you must take care of yourself. It has probably done you good to talk to me about this matter; later on, talk to Mrs Snow. She is a person to be trusted, and she is very fond of you. I am sorry, but I shall have to go now.'

I felt better for having talked to him, even though he had not offered advice, apart from telling me I should get some rest. This I did, and the following day I told Zillah part of the story; that the ayah had asked me to take Hanna. But did Zillah already know the true facts? After all, she had lived in Sadura all her life. Down at the bazaar they gossiped, and knew everything. But whether she knew or not, just then I did not feel I could discuss the matter with her.

With Mrs Snow, yes. Philip was no longer here; Hanna was the legacy which he had left behind. Sitting in Mrs Snow's bungalow, I listened to her talking about matters which she would never have mentioned while my husband was alive.

'Philip's mother was beautiful, but weak — seemingly unable to control her drinking. His father did not drink to excess, but he gambled, and there were other women. I think that had a lot to do with her drinking. The ayah came when Philip was a boy of about seven. She was a widow with a little girl, so he knew Sajoodaye from childhood, and when his mother died, his father just left the running of everything to the ayah. The upshot of it was, of course, that Sajoodaye had the run of the house, and played with Philip. He was never sent away to school, which would have been the best thing for him. He saw too much; his father kept an Indian woman for many years, and she visited the house. Philip was about twenty when his father died, but already there was talk of him and Sajoodaye. After all, she was living with the ayah, and doing light tasks around the house, and she was very beautiful, Adele.'

'Go on,' I said.

'Well, I've no doubt the ayah threw them together as much as possible, from the time Philip was eighteen or so. What could anyone expect from a boy brought up as he had been? Undoubtedly the ayah hoped to get him to marry Sajoo-daye, but her influence was not as great as that. When Sajoodaye was discreetly moved to Hush Hush Valley, I heard that she had given birth to a child, and that Philip was the father.

'His wild goings-on continued, and then he turned his attentions to Dorothy Forrester, when she came out here. She was clay in his hands, poor girl, but not so her parents. They knew too much about him, and gave him short shrift, with tragic results.'

'And then he went to England, and turned his attentions to me,' I said bitterly. 'I suppose I was just as silly as poor Miss Forrester.'

'My dear, when a young man is as handsome as Philip was, and as charming as he could be when he chose, it is not hard for romantic girls to fall in love with him. I knew you had been taken in; the more so when I learnt you were an orphan child, brought up in comfortable circum-stances, and well provided for. His motives were plain, added to the fact that most young men would find you attractive anyway. I thought perhaps he might have turned over a new leaf. I hoped so, for your sake.'

'But he didn't,' I said. 'And he didn't stop seeing Sajoodaye. He never would have done, either.'

'Perhaps you are right, Adele. Perhaps he was shallow; not to be trusted with women — perhaps he was all sorts of things. But he did care for Sajoodaye, and for Hanna, I suppose, in his own way. Try not to judge too harshly. His home life was far from ideal, remember.'

I sat there, and thought of Philip growing up with Sajoodaye. I thought of them when Philip had grown out of his childhood, and Sajoodaye was no longer a child, but a young woman. I thought of them laughing together, whispering together in the soft Telugu; loving together . . . and then I thought of Hanna.

'I don't know what to do about

Hanna,' I said. 'She is recovering well now, and will soon be out of hospital.'

'Well, she must go somewhere,' said Mrs Snow.

There was a short silence between us. 'I suppose she had better come to Lebanon for a while — until she is really well again. I've finished at the hospital now, so I shall have more time. And there is Zillah to care for her.'

Mrs Snow nodded her approval when I had finished speaking.

'We all did what we could to save Hanna,' she said. 'I hope it has all been worthwhile.'

A few days later, Zillah and I drove to the hospital, where I asked to see Dr Baxter.

'I've come to take Hanna,' I said, after we had exchanged greetings. He half smiled, then looked relieved.

'Ah, yes,' he said. 'Hanna. I've been expecting you some time this week.'

He had a word with a passing nurse, and shortly afterwards Hanna appeared, a very weak, frail looking Hanna now.

She seemed bewildered, and clung to the nurse's hand as she walked towards us. The chubbiness had gone from her face; the finely modelled features were revealed. She looked up at me, and suddenly I saw Philip's face in hers; Philip, with his eyes full of tears. It moved me to the bone; I could not speak for a moment; could scarcely bear to look at her.

'Goodbye, Hanna,' said Dr Baxter. 'I'll call in and see her,' he added, to me. Zillah and I got into the bullock-coach, with the sad, silent little girl between us.

17

With the resilience of childhood, Hanna soon regained her former strength. She began to chatter again, mostly in Telugu, but I did not encourage this. I wanted her to speak good English, although I had no objection to her speaking the native dialect too. I took her out of the somewhat garish clothes Sajoodaye had dressed her in, and now she wore white broderie anglaise, and her plaits were tied with ribbon, like any English girl. Gone were the heavy earrings, too. I allowed her to wear gold sleepers; the fact that her ears had been pierced while she was so young was no real disadvantage.

I wrote to my aunt and uncle, and told them I was taking care of a little orphaned Indian girl for a time. I sold the coffee plantation at Hush Hush Valley, and felt a tremendous sense of relief. Concerning the tile works, we were now more than holding our own with Giuseppe Fattorini's firm. We were turning out three times as many tiles as before; soon we would be doing better still. Chilwa Ragoobir had suggested we should try coal-firing, and this was the next thing we tackled.

Ernest Jones' uncle had died in the epidemic, and left his business to Ernest. I suggested he might like to sell it, and become my partner in the tile business. This he seemed very pleased to do.

'Hanna is a credit to you,' remarked Dr Baxter, when she had been out of hospital three weeks. 'It is hard to realize how ill she has been.'

'You look much less tired yourself,' I said.

'Yes, things are easier now. Sadura has certainly suffered this year, with floods and cholera.'

'And now it will soon be Christmas again.' We were standing on the verandah, watching Hanna play ball with Zillah.

'Yes, and another year.'

'I hear Miss Dysart has announced her engagement,' I said boldly. Mrs Snow had told me that Rosalie had met someone in Ootocamund, and that they planned to marry in the spring.

'Yes, so I understand.' Dr Baxter did not seem disposed to discuss the matter. I understood that Miss Dysart's parents had returned to Sadura, but that she was having a prolonged stay at her fiancé's home. I wondered what David Baxter thought about it. Had he cared for her; did he care for her? Or, after losing his wife, did he really only care for his work, and his patients?

'Have you made any further plans concerning Hanna — or the future?' he asked.

'Not really. My aunt and uncle would like me to go back to England.'

'It's very understandable,' was his non-commital comment. He then asked how the tile works was going on, and appeared to be pleased I was making a success of it.

'I hope things continue to go well for you,' he said, as he took his leave. I stood looking after him, thinking about our conversation. Yes, it had been a terrible year for Sadura. And for me. I thought of the disillusionments I had suffered; of the loss of my baby, and my husband.

Hanna stood poised with the ball in her hand.

'Wa-atch me, please,' she said carefully, in English.

'I'm watching,' I said, smiling. Seeing her play on the sunlit grass, I suddenly felt that I could never let her go. She too had suffered great losses over the past year. And what harm had she ever done anyone? Like her, I had been orphaned as a child, but I had never felt a sense of loss, as I had been taken and loved and cherished. I thought of what David Baxter had said when I was considering taking Hanna: 'An act of great charity — and courage'.

Did he really think so? Somehow, I wanted him to. Even though I was my own mistress now, and the tile works was doing well, I was not very happy. I had the companionship of Zillah, and I had the Snows, who loved me to take Hanna to see them. I was still friendly with the Radstocks, and several other couples in Sadura. But somehow things were not quite the same, as I was now an unattached woman. You were a single girl and then you got married. But even if you were only married for a short time, like me, you could never go back. Nothing could, or would, ever be the same again. Other feelings bewildered me, too. I had thought that to love as I had loved Philip was the only way; I had thought it must be at first sight; an all-consuming passion.

But was it possible that love could creep upon you slowly, half unrecognized at first, but always there? That you could learn to respect a man, and admire his character, before you actually fell in love with him? Suppose this happened, and the man in question was not interested? Suppose he was only being kind to you . . .

Deliberately I turned my thoughts away, and told Zillah and Hannah that we would go for a drive on to the ridge. But once up there, I remembered how I had gone there the first time on Dr Baxter's instructions. How long ago it seemed — an age, in fact. Now that Hanna was well, he had no further excuses to come to the house, I thought. Of course, he could come socially, but since Philip's death, he had not done that. One thing I knew now, though, and that was that Miss Dysart was engaged to someone else. So that had come to nothing — but why was I thinking like this? Did people have no control at all over their emotions, I asked myself.

But as often as I put thoughts of David Baxter out of my mind, they crept back as quickly. And so I carried my secret around; this sweet, tormenting thing which gave me no rest.

Soon we were making preparations for Christmas. Several invitations came my way; I reflected that in England I would have been considered extremely disrespectful to take part in any social occasion. Here, though, things were different.

The Snows gave a Christmas Eve dinner party, to which I was invited. I'd had a doll's house made for a Christmas gift for Hanna, and Mrs Snow had bought her a lovely doll. On Christmas Eve Hanna went to bed excited and happy; full of delightful expectations.

As Zillah helped me to dress that evening, I could not help remembering my first Christmas at Sadura. How kind everyone had been to me, thinking I would be homesick for England. I had been homesick for England many times, since then.

Zillah dressed my hair carefully, and helped me into a black lace gown. Back home in England, I would not have been wearing any ornament except jet, but I thought a string of pearls would not look amiss at Mrs Snow's dinner party. Since leaving the hospital the strain had left my face.

'You look very nice, Miss Adele,' said Zillah.

I was pleased when she said that, but when I got into the bullock-coach to drive to the Snows', I wondered rather sadly if it mattered how I looked. It seemed to me that since Philip's death, the attitude of the younger wives in Sadura had changed subtly towards me. In some curious, indefinable way, they seemed to have closed ranks against me. I supposed this was because I was no longer safely married off.

Yet Dr Baxter, as a young widower, was welcome everywhere. But then, of course, an unattached man was a social asset, unlike an unattached woman. As I went along in the bullock-coach, I thought about David Baxter, and how he would probably be at the Snows' tonight. And I thought of something else, which had been on my mind a great deal. I had imagined that if I could make a success of the tile works, and somehow get over Philip's death, and everything that had gone before, I would be content.

At least, I had thought that I would have achieved something, and that I would build a life here in Sadura, with Hanna to care for, and Zillah as a companion. But it was not working out as I had planned. I felt I could not continue to live in Sadura with any peace of mind, knowing that a certain man was living in the same place; a man I cared for deeply, but who did not return my feelings.

What was the use of going on, even though the tile works was doing better and better? When I arrived at the Snow's, however, Dr Baxter was not there. Mrs Snow lost no time in telling me why.

'Dr Baxter has just had word from England of his father's death. It is a great shock; I don't know what he will do now, I'm sure. His mother and unmarried sister are left; he will have to make a choice, and no mistake.'

'A choice?' I said, wishing my voice didn't sound so muffled. My heart was beating so quickly that I felt quite breathless.

'I believe they want him back home to carry on his father's practice. And no doubt plenty would deem it his duty.'

I could feel my face flushing with the shock of her words. He would have to make a choice! Oh, it was ironic. He, and not I might be leaving Sadura. A host of thoughts rushed through my mind, but I had to suppress them. After all, I was in company. Not surprisingly, though, Dr Baxter was the topic of the evening. Everyone agreed that he'd had a very bad year, with the floods, and the cholera epidemic.

'And now — this — right at Christmas.' Mrs Snow shook her head. Nevertheless, we drank our *chota-pegs*, and ate our way through the solid turkey and plum pudding which was served. Afterwards we played parlour games and sang carols. Mrs Snow said that although Dr Baxter had been asked to go home by his parents after his wife had died, he had thought he could be of more service staying in Sadura.

She added that he felt far too upset to come to the dinner party that evening, and anyway, perhaps it did seem a bit disrespectful. I felt as though I wanted to see him, though. I wanted to give him my condolences. At the same time, I hesitated to call at his bungalow. I would wait until Christmas was over.

Back at Lebanon, I spent a restless night. If David Baxter went back to England, I would no longer be troubled by his presence in Sadura. But suppose he did go back? Suppose I was left in this place without him? I thought of those terrible weeks following Philip's death, when I had so nearly booked a passage to England.

Dr Baxter had told me not to go back; not as a coward. And I had stayed and faced everything — yes, even the challenge of taking Hanna. Now it all seemed futile. I reflected that perhaps he, too, had felt like going home after his wife's death. But he had stayed, and done what was his duty in Sadura. Now I knew that he would weigh everything up carefully, and if he thought it was his duty to go back to England, he would go. I supposed, not without bitterness, that he had done his duty towards me as a doctor.

That was all it was, and why had I ever thought that it might have been more than that? At last I slept, and woke to a bright and sunny Christmas Day. Zillah and I exchanged gifts; a beautifully embroidered silk shawl from her, and from me to her, a delicate blouse which I had bought in Madras some time before. Then Zillah went home to spend the day with her parents. Hanna was delighted with her gifts; she danced around in the embroidered slippers Zillah had made for her.

Mr and Mrs Snow were coming to dinner on Boxing Day, but I had decided to have a quiet Christmas Day;

just myself and Hanna. Soon, I knew, she would need the companionship of other children; that was something else which I would have to think about. I played with Hanna, and strolled in the garden, and thought about David Baxter. And while I was thinking thus, Babwah announced that Dr Baxter was waiting to see me in the drawing room. Instantly I felt the blood rush to my face, and my hands seemed to go cold and clammy in spite of the warmth outside. I went slowly into the drawing room, to find him standing looking at the portrait of Philip's mother.

'Oh — Dr Baxter,' I exclaimed. 'I heard about your sad news at Mrs Snow's. I did not know whether to call and give you my condolences or not — ' I broke off. It was true that I had not known whether to call or not. In view of my feelings for him, I felt a hesitation, an embarrassment, about calling at his bungalow. How tired and drawn he looked.

'It has been a terrible shock,' he said.

'I felt quite unable to face a dinner party at the Snows' last night.'

'Do sit down,' I managed to say. 'I was so sorry to hear. Everyone was.'

He sat down, and I sat facing him. I could feel my heart beating painfully. Why had he come to see me? Why?

'My father's death was very sudden — quite unexpected. He has — had — a country practice in Gloucestershire, as you know. My mother and sister are very brave, and they are arranging for someone else to carry on the practice for the time being. They want me to go home, though.'

Hanna pattered into the room with her doll. I thought then that David Baxter and I had not exchanged Christmas greetings, but how could I wish him a happy Christmas under the circumstances? He smiled at Hanna. She gave him a shy glance through her fingers, giggled, and ran out of the room again.

'Play by yourself, Hanna,' I called after her. 'I'm talking to Dr Baxter.'

'Does she know what you are saying?' he asked.

'Probably not. But she is learning English words all the time.' We both fell silent, then. What did he want me to say? Why was he telling me that his mother and sister wanted him home?

'So you might be going back to England,' I said finally.

'I have to decide. It is very difficult. It is hard to know what is the right thing to do.'

'Only you can decide that,' I said at last. I was annoyed with myself for finding it so difficult to get the words out.

'You would not mind if I went back home, then?'

'It would scarcely matter if I did, surely?' Now I had thrown down a challenge.

'It would matter very much.' I realized then that he was in a very emotional state. All traces of professional manner had gone. I longed to throw myself into his arms and say that

348

whether he went or stayed, I wanted to be with him.

'Mrs Belvedere — Adele — this is very hard for me to say. I had intended to wait a while; to let you get over the shock of your husband's death before speaking. It has been so difficult for me — you are a young widow, and I am your doctor. I did not wish to rouse any gossip in the town. You must know I have a very high regard for you.'

'High regard?' I repeated, and my voice was almost a whisper.

'Adele — do you have any regard for me?'

Did I have any regard for him? The emotions welling up in me could not have been put into words. All I managed to reply was a whispered yes. The next moment we were locked in each other's arms; something I had dreamed of many times, but never really expected to happen. The joy of feeling his lips on mine was almost unbearable.

'Adele — dearest, sweetest, bravest

girl!' he said, a few minutes later. 'I've had to stand to one side, and watch you struggling on alone. And you've been so wonderful . . . You took over the mess which Philip had left in the tile works, and made a going concern of it. And then you came to the hospital, wanting to nurse during the cholera epidemic — I was so angry — '

'Why were you?' I asked.

'Because you were at risk, of course! You were just about the last person I wanted to volunteer to nurse — but you came.'

'Yes, I remember you didn't seem very pleased,' I said. We were sitting on the couch now, holding hands. 'You said I was too — something, but you never finished.'

'I was going to say you were too precious, but I dare not. I was worried the whole time you were there, and I knew you were still going to the factory every day, too. It was far too much for you. As for Hanna, I never thought you would take her into your home under the circumstances, but you did. Oh, Adele, if you only knew how I have thought about you, and worried about you, right from our first meeting.'

'You mean you liked me when I first came here?'

'I thought you were very nice, and I felt that things were going to be difficult for you. Somehow I wanted to protect you, and then I found that emotions were being stirred in me; something which I never thought could happen again after my wife died.'

'You were always very kind to me,' I said.

'I've been unhappy and tormented because I knew you were having such a rough time. When you first came here you seemed to have led such a sheltered life, but you were so eager to have a challenge from it.'

'I had my challenge from life, all right,' I said.

'Yes, but it's not over yet, by a long way.'

'What about Miss Dysart? Did you

ever care for her?'

'Not in the way I care for you. She's pretty, but her charms are very superficial. She's shallow and selfish, and I could never love a woman like that. If she had offered to nurse at the hospital, I would have respected her, but she never offered. Instead, she went off to the Nilgiris Hills, away from it all, and met someone else.'

'So you knew she wanted you?'

'She made it fairly obvious, and it was rather embarrassing, as her parents were clearly hopeful that I would rise to the bait. It required a great deal of tact to keep the situation under control. And when you were widowed, I could hardly rush round and tell you how I felt about you. I had to consider your good name, and of course, being your doctor complicated things. In any case, it would have been most indelicate on my part to talk about my feelings for you straight after Philip's death.'

'I suppose it would,' I said. 'I was very shocked at the time, anyway. I had to get over it as best I could.'

'And you got over it very bravely, too. I don't wish to talk about your husband now, but he was never worthy of you. I knew that right from the start. When you sent for me that morning, thinking he was ill after he had been drinking, I felt angry that you should have to put up with such things. But there was never anything I could do, Adele. I cared for you, and you were another man's wife. It's all been so difficult. I intended to wait until a year after Philip's death, before doing anything about the situation. But my hand has been forced, now. Dearest, if I decide to go back to England, will you sell the tile works, marry me, and come back with me?'

It had all happened so quickly that I felt as if my breath had been squeezed out of me. Marry David Baxter . . . sell the tile works . . . go back to England . . .

'And if you don't go back to England?' I asked slowly.

'Marry me just the same.'

'But you will go back! You have

already decided.'

'Yes,' he admitted. 'I feel I should, now. It means leaving these people, and not being able to help at the hospital. My parents wanted me to go back after I lost my wife, but I stayed and soldiered on, just as you did.'

'And now you think it's right for you to go.'

'When my wife died, my father was alive and well. I would have just been going back for my own sake. Now, it is different.'

'Yes,' I said. 'Your mother and sister need you. And I expect your father would have wanted you to carry on his practice.'

'Yes, he would. But could you face the idea of being the wife of a country doctor? I shall be very busy, and have many demands on my time — probably as many as I have here.'

'I don't mind that,' I said. 'There will be mutual love and trust. That is what is important. But there is Hanna to think of, too.'

'Yes, Hanna. What is to become of her?'

I thought about her . . . the ayah's granddaughter; the child of Philip's illicit union with an Indian girl. It would be easy to abandon her; take her to the convent, and pay the nuns to look after her. But could I do that? David drew me into his arms again.

'If you are prepared to keep Hanna, then I am,' he said. 'I know it's very unorthodox, and all the rest of it, but I don't mind. She is a child in need of a loving home, and we can give her that, Adele. When we leave Sadura, at least we can think we've done some good while we've been here.'

A strange feeling was rising within me, a feeling I had not experienced for a long time; happiness.

'Ernest Jones was left a business by his uncle; he sold it and put the money into the tile works — we became partners,' I said. 'I think I'll sell out to Ernest. I know it is in good hands with him.'

The prospect of going back to

England was suddenly intoxicating. I told David so.

'Going back now means you haven't run away from anything; not even from looking after Hanna,' he said.

'It's funny, you told me when I did go back, not to go back as a coward.'

'And you won't. But there will be many challenges to face when we do go back. There will be my mother and sister to comfort, and Hanna to explain away.'

'Yes, many challenges,' I agreed. 'But however many there are, we will face them together.'

For a few minutes neither of us spoke. I knew that David was sad about his father, yet happy about us. There was a kind of blurred joy about the rest of the day. As we made our plans for the future, we decided to wait a little while before mentioning them to our friends in Sadura. We both wanted to write home first.

I was so bubbling over with happiness and excitement, though, that I found it a difficult task to behave as though nothing had happened. I was eager to tell Mrs Snow and Zillah. However, in less than a week, Zillah, round-eyed, came to me, and told me that she had heard from Babwah the latest bazaar gossip.

They were saying that Dr Baxter was returning to England, but that he would be taking me too, as his bride.

'Oh, well, I intended to tell you about it, anyway,' I said, smiling. 'Yes, Zillah, it is true.'

I wondered for the hundredth time how they acquired their information at the bazaar, but I did not mind them gossiping now.

'Miss Adele, I am happy for you,' she said simply. 'He is a good man. Your aunt and uncle in England will be pleased.'

I smiled, thinking how once I would not have thought that love could come to anyone so slowly, and in such everyday conditions.

'Yes, they will be pleased, Zillah,' I said. And I added, half to myself: 'This time, they will be pleased.'

We do hope that you have enjoyed reading this large print book.

Did you know that all of our titles are available for purchase?

We publish a wide range of high quality large print books including:
Romances, Mysteries, Classics
General Fiction
Non Fiction and Westerns

Special interest titles available in large print are:
The Little Oxford Dictionary
Music Book, Song Book
Hymn Book, Service Book

Also available from us courtesy of Oxford University Press:
Young Readers' Dictionary
(large print edition)
Young Readers' Thesaurus
(large print edition)

For further information or a free brochure, please contact us at:
Ulverscroft Large Print Books Ltd.,
The Green, Bradgate Road, Anstey,
Leicester, LE7 7FU, England.
Tel: (00 44) **0116 236 4325**
Fax: (00 44) **0116 234 0205**

AS TIME GOES BY

Gillian Villiers

When Lally caretakes her grand-mother's croft in the wildest part of Scotland, she fully expects that she'll return soon, to a high-powered job in Edinburgh. Her scatterbrained sister Bel has other plans though, and Lally quickly finds the people and the place seeping into her soul. Or is it just one person, in the shape of new neighbour Iain? Torn between two worlds, Lally's decision will not only impact on herself, but also on everyone else around her.

A CERTAIN SMILE

Beth James

Freya has been made redundant and her high-flying boyfriend, Jay, is pressurising her to join him in London. But this would mean her leaving the place her heart lies — her home in the New Forest. And there are so many things to consider: her friends, her small cottage and her adorable, little dog Henri . . . and there's a certain dog walker with good legs and a friendly smile. Freya knows that she'd miss saying 'good morning' to him too.

CORY'S GIRLS

Teresa Ashby

Mark Jacobs returns to his home
town to settle old scores, but learns
that his ex-wife died two years
before. Emma, his daughter from
that marriage, and with whom he'd
lost contact, is settled and happy
with Cory Elliot, her stepfather, and
her two half-sisters. But Mark wants
her back, and when Cory has to go
abroad on business, he leaves the
girls with Katrina, who has to fight
to keep the family together for Cory
— the man she loves.

WHERE LOVE BELONGS

Chrissie Loveday

Lizzie Vale, Nellie Cobridge's youngest sibling, has to make a decision. What will she do with her life? Journalism excites her, but in 1938 it's not easy for a woman to get a job in this field, however bright and lively she is. Determined to succeed, she tries various schemes and tackles everything with enthusiasm. Fortunately, she has the support of a loving family when things go wrong. She meets Charlie and her future seems set. Or is it?